AVAILABLE DARK

Also by Elizabeth Hand

ELIZABETH HAND

AVAILABLE DARK

Small Beer Press
Easthampton, MA

Camera Lucida: Reflections On Photography by Roland Barthes, translation by Richard
Howard, translation copyright 1981 by Farrar, Straus and Giroux, Inc.

Small Beer Press
150 Pleasant St., # 306
Easthampton, MA 01027
info@smallbeerpress.com
bookmoonbooks.com
weightlessbooks.com
smallbeerpress.com

Distributed to the trade by Consortium.

Library of Congress Cataloging-in-Publication Data

Names: Hand, Elizabeth, author.
Title: Available dark / Elizabeth Hand.
Description: First Small Beer Press trade paper edition. | Easthampton, MA
    : Small Beer Press, 2021. | Summary: "Cass Neary finds herself drawn
    into the shadowy world of crime in Scandinavia's coldest corners"--
    Provided by publisher.
Identifiers: LCCN 2021026672 (print) | LCCN 2021026673 (ebook) | ISBN
    9781618731906 (print) | ISBN 9781618731913 (ebook)
Classification: LCC PS3558.A4619 A93 2021 (print) | LCC PS3558.A4619
    (ebook) | DDC 813/.54--dc23
LC record available at https://lccn.loc.gov/2021026672
LC ebook record available at https://lccn.loc.gov/2021026673

First printing 1 2 3 4 5 6 7 8 9 0

Text set in Centaur MT. Chapter numbers in Bell MT.
Cover © 2021 by Small Beer Press.
Printed on 30% Recycled Paper in the USA.

For Russell Dunn, 1958–2011,
soul mate, true artist, and fellow traveler in Reykjavík,
with love always

All those young photographers who are at work in the world, determined upon the capture of actuality, do not know that they are agents of Death.

—*Camera Lucida*, Roland Barthes,
translated by Richard Howard

Domine, libera nos a furore normannorum.
"Lord, save us from the rage of the Norsemen."

—Medieval prayer

Part One

1

There had been more trouble, as usual. In November I'd headed
north to an island off the coast of Maine, hoping to score an interview that might jump-start the cold wreckage of my career as a
photographer, dead for more than thirty years. Instead, I got sucked
into some seriously bad shit. The upshot was that I was now back
in the city, almost dead broke, with winter coming down and even
fewer prospects than when I'd left weeks earlier. I dealt with this
the way I usually did: I bought a bottle of Jack Daniel's, cranked my
stereo, and got hammered.

When I finally came to, it was dark. Sleet rattled against a
greasy window. In a corner of the apartment, a red light flashed
beside a stack of old LPs: I'd turned off my phone but forgotten
the answering machine. I lurched toward the blinking light, unsure
if it was early morning or night, yesterday or tomorrow.

"*Cass. What the hell did you do?*"

I rubbed my eyes, head throbbing.

"*. . . don't know how you got that photo of my mother, but you better call me fast. Sheriff Stone wants to talk to you, also that guy Wheedler from—*"

I hit erase and skipped to the next caller.

"*This is a message for Cassandra Neary from Investigator Jonathan Wheedler of the Maine State—*"

I erased that one, too, and all the rest without listening to them, just for good measure. Then I took a shower, waiting for ten minutes before the water pressure amped up to a scalding trickle. That's what thirty-odd years in a rent-stabilized apartment on the Lower East Side will buy you. I dressed—moth-eaten black sweater, ancient black jeans, steel-toed Tony Lamas, the battered leather jacket I'd bought at Goodwill decades ago—and went outside to forage for coffee.

It was night. Streetlamps gave off a smeared yellow glow. The financial meltdown hit my neighborhood hard—not that I had any sympathy for the unemployed hedge-fund assholes and fashion models who spent their afternoons whining into their iPhones in front of the Dries Van Noten store. Before the crash, this part of the city looked like a cross between a Downtown USA soundstage and the Short Hills Mall; instead of stepping over junkies, I maneuvered around rat-size dogs in Juicy Couture sweaters and designer diapers. Now I wondered how bad things would have to get before Jack Russell terriers showed up on the menu at Terrine.

But I couldn't afford to move. I'd been in the same place since the 1970s. The landlord had been trying to get rid of me for years; eviction notices had piled up in the weeks since I'd been gone, so I made a quick phone call to my father up in Kamensic Village.

"Talk to Ken Wilburn," he said. "He'll take care of it for you. Are you back from Maine, Cass? Any more trouble with that? Come home, and let's have dinner one night."

I said I'd think about it and hung up.

Tonight I kept my head down against the sleet and wished I owned a warmer coat. I passed a line of anorexics waiting to get into a restaurant specializing in downtown comfort food: mashed heirloom potatoes, truffle macaroni and artisanal cheese. As I walked by, one of the skinny girls laughed. I stopped, pivoting so that my boot's steel tip grazed her Bally Renovas.

"Did you say something?" Skeletor met my eyes and blanched.

"Didn't think so," I said, and kept going.

Back in the day, my nickname had been Scary Neary. Most of the people who called me that are dead now. No direct causal relationship, just bad drugs and worse luck. I'm nearly six feet tall, all speed-fused nerves and ragged dirty-blond hair, with a fresh scar beside my right eye, souvenir of my trip to Vacationland: a walking ad for Just Say No.

I skipped Starbucks in favor of the all-night Greek diner around the corner, found a booth in the back, ordered black coffee and a rib eye, rare. I was well into my steak when someone slid into the seat across from me.

"Hey, hey, hey. Cassandra Android."

I winced. Phil Cohen, onetime rock journalist manqué, now the mastermind behind a celebrity blog called *Early Death*. Phil was a local bottom-feeder, one or two steps above or below me on the social ladder, not that anyone was counting. He was also my most reliable source for speed.

I hadn't seen him since I'd been back. From the way he looked, alarmingly bright-eyed and bushy-tailed, the downturn in the economy hadn't hit his corner of Hoboken. Phil wasn't a bridge-and-tunnel guy; more just a tunnel guy, especially when you factored in his ratlike ability to scrounge a living in the dark.

"Phil. How's it hanging?"

"Not bad, not bad. Hey, I saw your photo got picked up by *The Smoking Gun.* Nice work. How the hell'd you do that?"

I pushed away my plate. "Fuck off, Phil."

Phil looked wounded. "I told that German editor to get in touch with you—the lady from *Stern*? They pay good money; I figured you could use a taste."

"You put her in touch with me?"

Phil nodded. He was fidgeting so much he looked like a life-size bobblehead. "Yeah, sure, how'd you think? Good thing your old man's a lawyer."

I glared at him and finished my coffee. Phil was the one who'd sent me to Maine; he'd lied about the interview he'd supposedly lined up, and lied about just about everything else, too. His connection turned out to be a photographer named Denny Ahearn, whose favorite subjects were decomposing bodies in trees. Long story short: Denny went overboard off the Maine coast and was now presumed dead. The story got some press but quickly ran out of steam since the killer was gone and the remains of only two victims had been recovered.

My own involvement in everything was a little shaky. I kept a low profile until I was safely back in New York, where an editor from the German tabloid weekly *Stern* had rung me a few days after my return.

"I so admire your work, Cassandra." Her voice had risen slightly. "Your photo book *Dead Girls*—that was brilliant. I was a big Bowie fan then, you know? We'd give you an exclusive...."

She had been disappointed when I told her I didn't have any photos of the serial killer or his victims. I'd been disappointed, too, when she named the figure they'd pay. Then I remembered the roll of film I'd shot on the island but hadn't yet developed.

It had been a weak moment for me. Most of my moments are like that. Finally I said, "You familiar with a photographer named Aphrodite Kamestos?"

"Aphrodite Kamestos? Of course. She's very well known here. Helmut Newton admired her work." The editor hesitated. "She just died, too, didn't she?"

I hadn't told her I'd watched Aphrodite die, or that I'd lied to the cops about it so I could avoid a conviction for voluntary manslaughter. I did a quick mental rundown of where I could cadge a few hours in a borrowed darkroom so I could process the film without anyone else seeing the images. "Yeah. I might have an image of her, kind of a memento mori. Like a death mask."

"A death mask?"

"Sure, you know. Something taken right after she died."

The editor had moaned. "Oh, that would be so great."

Now I stared across the table at Phil. "Yeah, good thing my old man's a lawyer. So, you got anything in that little black bag for me?"

Phil's eyes rolled back in his head like he was communing with the spirit world. "Focalin."

I stuck my hand under the table so he could drop a Baggie into it.

"You'll like this, Cass. Nice and easy, timed-release, no edge. And probably I shouldn't say this, 'cause I'd hate to lose your business, but you could see your doctor, he'd give you a scrip. Then you could get your health insurance to pay for it. Some Zoloft wouldn't kill you, either."

"Phil. Do I look like I have fucking health insurance?"

"Good point. Here, you want this?" He set a tiny glassine envelope on the table, then flicked it at me. It landed on my lap. "Touchdown."

"What is it?"

"Crystal meth. Very pure, Cass; we're talking Pellegrino, Fiuggi, all that shit. No one else wants it these days, but this is the stuff. Guy who used to be in the refrigerant industry, he still cooks with Freon. He's got a nice little stash of CHCs, but there ain't no more where this came from. I'll give you a deal on it, Cassie. As a Christmas present."

"Christmas is over, Phil. But yeah, I'll take it." I peeled off a few bills to cover my meal, handed him a couple more, then stood. "Later."

He pulled my plate over and began to eat the rest of my steak. "Yeah. Write if you get work."

I walked back to my apartment, taking care that my cowboy boots didn't send me flying as I navigated the slush-choked sidewalk. I'd taken the *Stern* payment and had the boots resoled, but they still weren't shit in bad weather. The rest of the money had gone to cover unpaid bills, plus a small retainer set aside for Ken Wilburn so I could hang on to my place for another year or two.

And that was it. I'd already gotten fired from my longtime job at the Strand Bookstore, no great loss save for the five-finger discount I'd exercised over the years, building up a small library of expensive photography books. Even that was a victim to changing times, as store security had amped up to TSA levels, with metal detectors and bag checks before you set a foot on the floor.

But being broke wasn't really the worst thing. I'd spent most of my adult life as a burned-out underachiever, working in the Strand's stockroom, drifting from one bed to another. For a few years in my twenties I'd been able to trade on the flash success I'd had with *Dead Girls*, my first and only book of photographs. Everything since then had pretty much been aftermath.

Still, through it all I'd always had the Lower East Side and the shadowy image behind my retinas of what it had once been: that 3:00 a.m. wasteland I'd fallen in love with when I was eighteen, shattered syringes and blood on the lip of a broken bottle, guitars and drunken laughter echoing through an alley where kids nodded out while I shot their pictures. The way something was always moving at the corner of my eye; the way the city was always moving, morphing into something new and terrible and beautiful.

The terror I knew on a first-name basis. On my twenty-third birthday I was raped outside CBGB. The scars are so old, as the song goes, now part of a faded tattoo I got on my lower abdomen to hide the bloody scrawl left by a zip knife. But even so, I could still sometimes find the silver-nitrate city inside the real one, if the light was right and I'd had enough to drink, scored enough amphetamine to make my heart keep pace with the strobe of my camera's flash.

Now all that beauty was gone. I was too old and too broke to go looking for it elsewhere. I'd spent too much time alone, skating on alcohol and speed, not noticing the ice beneath me was rotten and the water killing cold.

The last person who said she loved me died on 9/11. I'd forgotten what she looked like. I was a burned-out, aging punk with a dead gaze, a faded tattoo, and a raw red scar beside one eye. In Maine I'd spent more time with other people than I had in years, maybe decades. There'd been a few moments when I'd held my battered camera and felt the way I did long ago, when I first stood in a

7

darkroom and watched another world bloom on the emulsion paper in my hands.

But that feeling was gone; that world. Since my return to New York, I'd begun to have night terrors, paroxysms of pure horror, where I would see a black figure above my bed, smiling as he reached for my throat, and woke to my own muffled screams, heart pounding like a fist inside my chest. I felt strung out, wasted in every sense of the word, terrified of sleep and almost as afraid to leave my squalid apartment. The edge where I'd lived for all these years was starting to look like a precipice. I figured it was a good time for a short visit with my father. I crashed for a few hours back in my apartment, woke, and swallowed a couple of Phil's white tablets; then headed to Grand Central to catch the first train to Kamensic.

2

The sleet that had made the city a skating rink turned to heavy snow when the train left Valhalla. By the time we pulled into Kamensic, I could see cars sliding across the southbound lane of the Saw Mill, and the beacons of emergency vehicles flashing like Christmas lights in the distance.

My father was waiting for me at the station. I'd called him before I left the city; he's an early riser, up before dawn even at the darkest time of year.

"Hello, Cass." He dipped his head to graze my cheek in a kiss, zipped his old L.L.Bean parka, then headed toward the parking lot.

"You didn't have to pick me up. I told you I could walk."

"Did you see it's snowing?" he asked, and we drove home.

Since the late 1960s my father has been the Kamensic Village magistrate, holding court on alternate Tuesdays and otherwise tending to a few old legal clients from his basement office in the house where I grew up.

The town had turned into a junk-bond trader's Disneyland since then. Most of the old colonial houses were now trophy second homes, or teardowns turned McMansions, empty save for the shriek of alarm systems set off by barking dogs, and a seasonal army of workers bused in from Stamford, wiry Latino men wielding lawn mowers, leaf blowers, and, this morning, snowblowers. Martha Stewart owned a $20-million cottage outside town, where she'd spent the last few years trademarking the name *Kamensic* for a line of outdoor furniture that cost as much as a semester at a Baby Ivy.

I hated going back, though I was cheered to see the storm had knocked a giant oak onto the most recent addition to a neighbor's house.

"Their alarm was going all night," my father said as we pulled into the drive. "I tried calling the owners in the city, but they won't pick up their phone."

"They're getting a lot of snow inside their new addition."

My father smiled. He's the only person in Kamensic who still mows his own lawn.

We ate breakfast, then read *The New York Times*. We didn't talk all that much, but I was used to that. My mother died in a car crash when I was four, an accident that left her impaled on the steering wheel and me rigid and staring, wide-eyed, when the police found the wreckage. Since then, my father's basic rule of thumb has always been that as long as I didn't get hauled in front of his court, he wouldn't ask too many questions.

"How was Maine?" he asked.

"Cold."

"Did you stop in Freeport?"

"No."

He stood and gathered a pile of papers from the sideboard. "I have a few things to take care of downstairs." He started for the door to the basement, stopped, and turned. "Oh, Cass—this came for you." He pulled an envelope from the sheaf of papers and handed it to me. "You're not in default on your student loan, are you?"

This was a joke. I'd dropped out of NYU in my freshman year, which was about the last time I'd received any mail at this address. I looked at the envelope, puzzled. "When did it come?"

"Last week."

He went downstairs. I walked into the living room, eerily blue-lit from the snow whirling outside, sat, and stared at the envelope. Thin, airmail-weight paper, with my name and address written in black cursive ballpoint ink. Painstaking, almost childish handwriting, like someone trying to make a good impression. I felt the tiniest frisson, somewhere between dread and exultation.

I knew that writing—or had known it, once.

But the memory was gone now. The oversize stamp showed a snow-covered expanse with bands of green and violet rippling above it.

ISLAND 120

No return address. Who the hell did I know in Iceland? I squinted, trying to read the postmark.

REYKJAVIK.

The fragile paper tore when I opened it. Inside was a newspaper clipping in Icelandic. It featured a grainy black-and-white image of a fir-tipped islet with a caption beneath: PASWEGAS, MAINE, USA. I scanned the column until I recognized my name—CASSANDRA NEARY.

11

So I had a fan in Iceland; someone who read *Stern,* maybe. I frowned and examined the envelope again.

There was something else inside. I removed it carefully.

It was a photo of a naked teenage boy, sprawled on an unmade bed. Grainy black and white, 4×6, the edges curled and faintly browned with age. He was wiry, his chest nearly hairless, half-erect cock shadowed in his crotch. His hair fell to his shoulders and framed an androgynous face: white skin, curved ridge of cheekbone, small chin, full lips, and slightly prominent teeth.

But it was those bruised eyes that killed me, eyes so deep set they seemed lined with kohl. He had his hands locked behind his head and gazed at the viewfinder dead-on. Not a come-hither stare but a wary, challenging look, as though he were debating whether to lunge across the bed and smash the camera or pull the photographer down beside him on the gray sheets.

I knew how that particular argument ended. I knew how they all ended, because I'd been the one behind the camera.

"Fucking hell," I whispered. "Quinn."

Thirty years ago I'd stood beside that bed, in a room less than a mile from where I sat now. I'd shot roll after roll of Tri-X film, always pictures of Quinn O'Boyle, sometimes clothed but mostly naked; before we fucked, afterward, during. Quinn hunched over his old Royal upright typewriter, or nodding out, or poring over his dog-eared paperback of *The Return of the King.* Walking toward the Kamensic train station, slumped in a booth at the Parkway Diner. Quinn and me standing side by side, a flare where my camera's flash ignited the mirror that held our reflection. I'd ridden my bike to Mount Kisco to have the film processed at a grimy store whose proprietor specialized in "art photos," an old man who chain-smoked Larks and smelled like Sen-Sen. He only raised an eyebrow once, when he handed me back my contact sheets and said, "Aren't you kinda young for this?"

I turned the picture again and stared at the boy on the bed. I'd shot scores of photos. Hundreds, maybe. I'd stashed them in a wooden Chivas Regal box, but I hadn't seen it, or any of the photos, in almost three decades. I'd ransacked my room, the house, the basement. I never found them.

And Quinn—he'd also disappeared. The two of us had broken into a local drugstore one night when we were eighteen. We weren't caught. My little stash of Quaaludes saw me through my first year in the city, but by then Quinn had taken off upstate with a woman he met in Harlem one night. I was sick with desire for him, sick with rage, and terrified that I'd never shoot another photo worth looking at. I channeled it all into speed and the photos that eventually became *Dead Girls.* Around the time the book came out, I heard that Quinn had gotten popped for breaking into another drugstore up in Putnam County. He wrote to me from his parents' house, where he awaited sentencing, desperate pleading letters, handwritten or typed on lined paper torn from a composition book. Sometimes he sent fragments of a story he was working on. Once he sent a Quaalude, crushed in transit to a smear of pink powder.

I never wrote back. When he left me, I felt as though someone had jabbed my eyes with a needle. Nothing looked the same after that. I'd honed my sense of damage on him, the bitter pheromone I'd inhale as I watched him hold a spoonful of brown powder over a gas flame till it melted into the chamber of a syringe. For years after he was gone, I still carried that acrid taste in my mouth and the afterimage of his eyes, the pupils swallowed by junk.

I had assumed he was dead. His family had moved to the Midwest. I never tried to track him down.

What the hell was he doing in Iceland?

"Who's your letter from?"

I started as my father came into the room behind me. "No one. Just a newspaper article." I slipped the photo back into the envelope and pocketed it, tossed the news clipping into the wastebasket. "Has anything else come here for me?"

"Not a thing. I need to head over to the town office for a few hours. Are you staying for dinner?"

I stared out to where trees and stone walls dissolved into a formless blur. "No. I have to get back. Can I catch a ride with you to the station?"

While he got ready I went upstairs to my old room. Nothing there remained of me, no posters or books, no clothing or record albums; just my old bed, now sanitized with a white chenille spread and white pillows. I took out Quinn's photo, stood by the window, and stared at it. I felt a shiver of apprehension, a dark flash at the corner of my eyes, the lingering odor of scorched metal and blood.

3

The train was delayed because of snow. By the time I finally slogged back to my apartment, it was dark. I ate some tuna fish out of the can, then settled at my ancient computer to Google Quinn O'Boyle.

I came up with nothing. No one in Iceland, no one who looked or sounded like the man he might have become, the kind of guy who'd send a nude photo of himself to the teenage lover he hadn't seen in thirty years.

After a few minutes I gave up and scanned my e-mail. Nothing but spam.

Or almost nothing.

From: derrabe@norwaymi.com
Subject: Photo Op

Dear Cassandra Neary,

I am a longtime admirer of your masterpiece *Dead Girls* and saw your photograph of the late Aphrodite Kamestos in *Stern.* I am wondering if you would have interest in a brief professional consultation of some photos I am considering as an acquisition. . . .

Another weirdo. I started to delete it but stopped when I scanned the end of the message.

I would of course not expect you to perform this service gratis and would be happy to discuss it with you as regards generous remuneration for your time.

With respectful regards,

Anton Bredahl

I had better luck Googling this guy. He was the owner of an Oslo club called Forsvar, a former air-raid shelter that specialized in industrial music, death metal—stuff like that. From its Web site, it seemed like a lot of his customers hadn't gotten over the bad news about Ian Curtis. The rest looked like they'd just come from Anvil's anniversary tour. There were a few underlit photos of the club's interior but none of its owner.

I sat for a minute and wrote my response.

Anton,
Sure, let's discuss.
CN

I hit reply and went to pour myself a drink. When I returned, another message had already popped onto the screen.

Can you talk now? What is your phone #?

I stared out a gray window glazed with sleet. I finished my Jack Daniel's, thought *What the hell,* and typed in my number. A minute later the pho ne rang.

"This is Anton Bredahl."

"You're quick."

"I am more comfortable in conversation. First let me say I know your work—I have a copy of *Dead Girls.*"

"You and twenty-five other people."

He laughed. The connection wasn't great, a cell phone or Skype. He sounded younger than me—late thirties, maybe. Not much of an accent.

"Yes, it was hard to find," he went on. "An American friend told me about it. I bought it from a dealer a few years ago, someone in Oslo here who specializes in photography. It is a valuable book now, did you know that?"

"So I've heard."

"I paid one hundred and forty euros. The exchange rate was not so good, so—it was expensive. I should have waited until now, right?" He laughed again. "Someone should bring it back into print. It's a good book. That is how I recognized the photo in *Stern.* The same eye, I thought. It's good you're taking photos again."

"It'd be better if I was getting paid for it."

This time he didn't laugh. I finished my drink, wondering if I'd pissed him off.

"Yes, that is why I wanted to talk to you. I collect photographs."

"The *Stern* photo isn't for sale." I'd already stuck the negs in various books around the apartment, a half-assed attempt at hiding them. "None of my stuff is for sale, sorry."

"Oh, no." He sounded slightly embarrassed—for me, I realized as he continued. "Actually, I was wondering if you would be interested in looking at some photos and perhaps assessing them. Not my own photos—I'm not a photographer. Photos I am thinking of acquiring for my collection. I think there is some overlap in our taste."

"I kinda doubt that." I paced to the kitchen and poured another drink. "I haven't done anything since *Dead Girls*; you know that, right?"

"You did the *Stern* photo."

I had a spike of paranoia—he was a cop, the whole *Stern* thing had been a setup to implicate me in Aphrodite's death—but before I could hang up, he added, "Joel-Peter Witkin—I bought his work very early on. But it is his later photos that I find most beautiful—the ones of the cadavers, before they became too camp. I have a number of other photographs as well. Weegee, but also—well, my taste is fairly . . . esoteric. You understand?"

"Right." I relaxed and knocked back the whiskey. "Yeah, I sure do."

"Esoteric" has roughly the same relation to my camera work as "erotica" has to porn. This guy liked the photographic equivalent of rough trade—very rough trade, as in dead people. Witkin's most notorious pictures center around cadavers and various body parts gleaned from morgues and hospital freezers, rearranged and posed to evoke images like the martyred St. Sebastian, or surrealist tableaux that would give Buñuel the creeps.

Bredahl said, "You like Witkin's work?"

"Yeah. Some. The stuff that isn't trying too hard. It's beautiful."

"Isn't it?" His voice lifted. "So many people don't perceive how beautiful it is, the way he sees the world. That image of the severed heads kissing is sublime."

"I wouldn't hang it in my kitchen. But yeah, it's an amazing photo."

Joel-Peter Witkin was definitely a somewhat esoteric taste. Also an expensive one: After Jesse Helms denounced his work as degenerate, prices went through the roof.

All this made me wonder why Bredahl needed me to take a look at his photos. Witkin was way out of my league. If I hadn't flamed out in the 1970s, you might have found my name alongside his in the Wikipedia entry for transgressive art. As it was, I was barely a footnote. Still, I needed to eat. Or drink, anyway.

"So you want me to authenticate some stolen Witkin photos? I'm not a curator; I couldn't give you an estimate of how much they're worth or anything like that. But I could take a look at them."

"No." Bredahl paused for such a long time I thought the line had gone dead. "I don't want you to make an assessment of their value. I would like your opinion. I would like the use of your eyes, as a consultant, someone who will tell me whether these pictures are authentic or not. The particular sequence I would like you to review is not by Witkin. These are a slightly different kind of photo. As I said, very specialized, very—"

"Esoteric?"

"Yes. Some people might find them quite offensive."

"Listen, if this is some kind of kiddie porn—"

"No, of course not. But I must be—how do I explain? Circumspect. More than anything, I need to know if these photos are . . . authentic. You understand?"

"No." I swallowed the rest of my Jack Daniel's. "Look, I don't think this is going to work, okay? I have to—"

"I will cover all your expenses. Not in Oslo—Helsinki. And I will pay you six thousand euros."

I did the math in my head.

"Yeah, well, okay," I said.

"I'll arrange your flights. Is Thursday too soon?"

This was Wednesday. "Thursday?" I'd only been out of the country once, on an ill-fated trip to Belize. I frantically rifled my desk until I found my passport under a stack of ancient contact sheets. It was valid for another year. "Yeah, Thursday's great."

"Excellent. Now . . ."

I gave him the info he needed to arrange the flight.

"I'll e-mail you a link so you can look at a few things in my archive." I heard him light a cigarette, then inhale. "What I've put online, anyway. Probably it would be good not to share this with your friends."

I promised not to share it with my friends. Not that I have any. I had a sudden bad thought.

"Hey—you know a guy named Phil Cohen?"

"Phil Cohen? No."

"You're sure?"

"I think so. Is that a problem?"

"No. That's good. I'll wait for your e-mail," I said, and hung up.

4

Bredahl worked fast. In moments another e-mail arrived: a link to his Web page, with instructions to click on the icon of a raven, follow that link to a second site, where I should click on a rainbow, then on to a site where I should sign in pseudonymously and, after receiving a password, type in the long string of numerals that he provided.

All this took me to Anton's site. No photo, no personal information of any kind; just a white screen crowded with totemic-looking animals—wolves, whales, puffins, eagles, serpents. It took me a minute to find the raven, which brought me to a page that looked as though it had been created by a fifth-grade girl, all pastel clip art of unicorns and fairies. I clicked on the rainbow, which drew up a spreadsheet for the accounting office of a furniture company. There was a place to log in, and I did, under Cam Lucida. I entered the numeric password and found myself staring at a screen deep in the darkweb.

Plukke rune

I hesitated, then clicked an icon. Up popped a black-and-white daguerreotype of a wizened infant, swaddled in a christening gown and lying on a bed. The baby's eyes were shut, its tiny hands like a dead bird's claws.

A Victorian postmortem daguerreotype. Photographers cranked them out in the early days of studio work, memento mori that were handed to the grieving family for display in the parlor or family Bible. They were highly collectible, though not particularly valuable: Too many had been produced by anonymous photographers eager to make a buck when the art was still new. I couldn't afford to turn down Bredahl's money, but this kind of macabre kitsch was definitely not to my taste.

I clicked another link. Up popped a second postmortem photo, of a dark-skinned young woman lying in a coffin surrounded by tall vases of white roses. Billows of lace and satin frothed down the sides of the casket; her clasped hands held an immense bouquet of white lilies. She'd been buried in her wedding dress.

James Van Der Zee, 1920s

This was more like it. Van Der Zee was a black photographer who shot tens of thousands of photos in the early twentieth century. I had a copy of his *Harlem Book of the Dead* I'd nicked from the Strand when it first came out. That book would cost you five bills and change now. Van Der Zee was almost a hundred when he died, and kept shooting nearly to the end—celebrity portraits, mostly. I could only guess what one of his early Harlem photos would go for.

If this online archive was for real, Bredahl owned several. He also owned a bunch of photos by Weegee, the notorious New York newspaper photographer who earned his nickname because of a seemingly supernatural ability to arrive at a murder scene while the corpse was still warm, usually before police or ambulance.

I had one of Weegee's books, too, but I'd never seen the pictures that Bredahl showed here. A naked woman splayed upon the boardwalk at Coney Island, torso split from throat to groin so her skin flapped like soiled bedsheets. A headless man slumped on a barstool, his spinal column protruding from a polka-dot shirt. A black Chihuahua lapping at a pool of blood beside a severed hand. There were also several Witkins I didn't recognize, as well as contraband photos from the FBI's Body Farm that showed cadavers scattered across a bucolic landscape.

I now had a good suss on Bredahl's esoteric taste. Also of how much discretionary income he had. Enough to invest in legitimate works, some of them one of a kind, and to subsidize runners who specialized in black-market pictures that had probably been stolen. I should have asked for more money.

I wrote him an e-mail.

Interesting site. Where'd you find those Weegees?

Bredahl's reply was terse.

www.saatavissatumma.com

I thought the URL might be for a private auction site or gallery. Instead, the link took me to a screen pulsing with silvery light.

Astua Sisään. Enter.

I clicked.

There were no Weegees here. Dreamy, vaguely familiar images filled the screen: bruised women sitting in office cubicles on an ice floe; square-jawed men in eyewear forged of rusty nails; a line of solemn blond children marching across a rocky beach, arms laden with leafless birch twigs. The locations were arctic, even when the models wore acid-green shantung sheaths or skirts of distressed chiffon: ice-locked lakes, barren tundra, evergreens so thick with snow they resembled alabaster topiaries. In one image, disheveled women in fur leggings and camisoles harnessed reindeer to a sled piled with raw meat. The photos were shot on film, not digitally; a highly saturated palette of indigo, silver, ochre deepening to the coppery black of dried blood; a pure, snow-blind white nearly impossible to capture without washing out the faces of the models.

That ethereal white twigged it for me. The site belonged to the Finnish fashion photographer Ilkka Kaltunnen. He'd been a prodigy during the late 1990s, when he was only in his twenties, and had a flash of notoriety for a *Vogue* shoot where the models all appeared to have died of heroin overdoses in a sauna. He'd also shot album covers for a couple of obscure Scandinavian bands excoriated for their involvement in church burnings and other satanic hijinks in Norway and Sweden.

25

Those scenes were mostly off my radar. I knew Kaltunnen for his real work. Among serious photographers, Kaltunnen was noted for that signature white: a burst of radiance in a model's eyes or the silver clasp of a bracelet; a brilliant, malign flare no one else could replicate in a darkroom.

His heroin chic seemed a little off-topic for Bredahl's collection. No rough edges. No dead people.

And I was no longer in the darkweb. I scanned Kaltunnen's site and found more fashion pictures, none more recent than 1999; a few music videos; some bleak winter landscapes and panoramic black-and-white shots of an industrial waterfront.

Nothing seemed to fit Bredahl's remit. I returned to his archive, searched for anything credited to Kaltunnen.

Nada. I was still brooding when the next message from Bredahl arrived. I checked the time: If he was in Oslo, this guy kept late hours. The e-mail consisted of another complicated set of links into the darkweb.

"Holy shit." I refilled my glass, staring at what was on the screen.

It was a night photo, deep focus, color—an expanse of jagged, snow-drifted rocks, spare and bleached as the surface of the moon. Near the center, a young man lay on his back as though sunbathing. He wore a candy-striped parka with a white fur hood, black jeans, and black motorcycle boots. He was thin and had long black hair.

But it was impossible to get a clear look at his face, because a window, frame and all, had been smashed against it. Broken glass shone like ice on the parka; the stripes on his parka were streaks of blood. A hank of black hair was snarled around a splintered muntin. A spar of wood split his lower jaw so that it gaped open, tongue lolling between crimson teeth. His cheek had been pierced by a triangular piece of glass. Where it split his flesh, a tiny sun glowed, the most brilliant thing in that surreal, glittering world. There was a single word on the screen:

Gluggagægir

If it was fake—Photoshop or a still from some slasher movie—it was the most convincing fake I'd ever seen. If not, it was the most beautifully composed crime-scene photo on Earth. I hadn't followed Kaltunnen's career since he'd retired from the fashion world, but it had always been a point of pride for him to work only with available light, and he'd broken contracts rather than allow magazines to retouch his work.

That radioactive flare was his signature; but how had he gotten it on a moonless night, working without a flash, with no available light? It was impossible.

And who kills someone with a window?

If this photo was for real, Kaltunnen would be crazy to leak it, unless he was up for a long afternoon with the police. Bredahl would be crazy to buy it.

And I was crazy to be looking at it. Before I could quit the screen, my phone rang again. It was Anton.

"Forget it," I said.

"Oh, he didn't kill him; he didn't kill any of them."

" 'Them'?"

Bredahl made a dismissive sound. "Did Weegee kill the people in his photographs?"

"So this is, what? A crime-scene photo? A fashion shoot?"

"You really do have a good eye, Cassandra."

"For what?"

"You recognized it as Ilkka's work."

"You just sent me a link to his goddamn Web site."

"Yes, but most people would have been looking at the people and the clothes. And you knew this photo was authentic. You recognized the light."

"Kaltunnen was famous for his light; *CameraArts* did a cover story on it twelve years ago."

"Yes, and you remember that, too." He sounded gleeful. "I've made your flight arrangements. Direct to Helsinki tomorrow evening; you'll arrive early Friday morning. The bus goes from the airport to the train station; you can take a cab or bus to Ilkka's house. I will arrange to have half your fee delivered to you there; the rest I will give you after I have completed my own transaction with Ilkka. You must be certain that all the photos are original and that the sequence is complete: There should be six of them. If you incur any other expenses, let me know; also how you would like the rest of your fee to be paid."

"You're sending me to Ilkka Kaltunnen?"

"Yes, of course. I envy you. No one has seen this sequence, not even me. Only that one photo. His wife is very nice. What is your mobile number?"

"I don't have a fucking cell phone."

"Get one in Helsinki. The whole country is fucking cell phones!"

He laughed, and the line went dead.

5

I awoke early the next afternoon, feeling like I'd fallen out a fifth-floor window. My computer was still on, but the last e-mail Bredahl had sent me was gone. I must have deleted it, out of drunken panic or spite. Among the usual spam I found a flight itinerary, an electronic voucher for my e-ticket, and Ilkka Kaltunnen's address and phone number in Helsinki.

I cursed myself for deleting that message. I tried in vain to remember the URL, checked my browser's history and clicked on the link. It was no longer valid. Neither were any of the links that had brought me to the darkweb the night before. If it hadn't been for the e-ticket and itinerary, the whole thing might have been the backwash from another bad hangover.

But given my recent phone messages, it seemed like a good time to get the hell out of Dodge. I downed some ibuprofen and a couple of Focalin and scrambled around the apartment to pack. I didn't have much in the way of warm clothes: a few long-sleeve black T-shirts and worn black cashmere turtlenecks, a bulky black sweater, two pairs of skinny black jeans, an old striped Breton shirt, some socks that weren't too threadbare. I went to an ATM and withdrew what remained of my cash. I briefly considered splurging for a warmer coat but didn't want to use up my meager credit. Instead I bought a pair of cheap leather gloves and a knit watch cap from a street vendor, along with a fake Burberry scarf.

Back in the apartment, everything fit into the same beat-up satchel I'd been carrying around since I was a teenager. I transferred the Focalin into an empty prescription bottle that had last held antibiotics, tossing in some Vicodin to even things out; stuck Phil's glassine envelope of crank into a little Baggie with some ground coffee, to throw off drug dogs at the airport, and shoved the Baggie through a hole in the lining of my leather jacket. Then I found my camera, the ancient Konica my father had given me on my seventeenth birthday.

Over the years I could, intermittently, have afforded a better rig. Phil Cohen never stopped giving me shit for not upgrading to digital.

But the Konica got the job done. I replaced the battery and made sure the flash was charged, and stuck the zoom into the satchel with everything else. I got out the ziplock bag of film I kept in the freezer, removed some rolls of Tri-X, and packed them, setting aside one. A camera's like a gun—no good unless it's loaded and in your hand when you need it.

I printed out the information Bredahl had sent me, then deleted all his e-mails and cleared my browser's history. They could still be dug out of the hard drive by a cop or dedicated hacker, but I hoped my anxiety was a function of alcohol and prescription amphetamines.

If it wasn't, I wanted to make my electronic trail a little harder to follow. I pulled on my cowboy boots—not the best gear for Helsinki, but all I had—grabbed my leather jacket, started for the door, and hesitated.

On the desk beside my computer was the envelope from Quinn. I pulled out the photo and stared at it; then I stuck it in my bag, and went to catch the bus to JFK.

By the time I got to the airport, I was vibrating from caffeine and Focalin and shaky because I hadn't had a drink since leaving my apartment. The TSA guy gave me the hairy eyeball. But there didn't seem to be an APB out on my passport, so once past security I loaded the roll of Tri-X into my camera, exchanged some of my dollars for euros, and found the duty-free shop. I knew two things about Finland: It was cold, and alcohol cost more than cocaine. I bought a bottle of Jack Daniel's for the trip, then found a bar to kill time until my flight was called. Once on board I wedged myself against the window. I swallowed a Vicodin, pulled the watch cap over my eyes, and passed out.

It was dark when I left New York, dark when the flight landed at 6:00 a.m. in Helsinki; dark when I filed through Border Control and got my passport stamped by a guy who looked like his last job had been checking IDs in Lothlórien. Two hours later, when I finally stumbled from a bus into the slush-covered street in front of the railroad station in Helsinki, it was still dark.

6

The exterior of the Saarinen-designed train station was flanked by ominous colossi that looked like they'd really do a number on your head if you were tripping for the first time. The wind was freezing and smelled like the sea. I shivered and pulled up the collar of my leather jacket, dodging thin, silent people in black on their way to work, and looked for a cab in the stream of buses and cars whipping past.

After a few minutes a battered Audi with a taxi sign pulled over. The door opened and a man tumbled onto the sidewalk. He landed on his hands and knees and lifted his head to stare at me, dazed.

I stepped over him and ducked inside. The cab jolted off before I closed the door. Music shrieked from a tinny speaker, some kind of opera. The driver yelled something at me. I shook my head and pointed vehemently at the radio. He made a face, but turned it down.

"*Mihin mennään?*"

"I don't speak Finnish. I'm going here."

I handed him the piece of paper with Ilkka Kaltunnen's address on it. He glanced at it, then at me.

"You could walk, you know. It's not far."

"Or you could just drive me."

The car shot forward then jerked to a halt at a stoplight. My head slammed the seat behind me, but before I could steady myself, we were off again. I grabbed the door handle and felt a stab of sympathy for the guy kneeling back in front of the train station.

The driver gave me a suspicious look in the rearview mirror. "You don't like Wagner?"

"Yeah, sure, I love Wagner. Just not so loud."

"*Das Rheingold.* Good for the drive to work. You American?" I gave him a curt nod. "I've been to Disneyland five times. I love America. You been to Disneyland?"

"No."

"You should go."

"It's on my life list." I read the name on his ID—William Lindblad. "You Swedish?"

"Swedish Finn. Like Tove Jansson. Who do you know in Ullanlinna?"

"Friend of a friend."

"You have rich friends."

I stared out at a stretch of high-end stores and restaurants, sleek Art Nouveau buildings alongside blocky Soviet-style housing. A metallic-blue sheen clung to everything, toxic by-product of the nearly sunless morning. It all looked familiar in an odd way, like a northern American city that had been Photoshopped. Yet the light seemed unworldly, as though I viewed the streets through a lens that filtered out the sun and tinted the world gunmetal blue.

The car made a sharp turn, dodging an old woman in layers of bright clothing and a long knitted cap. The smell of the sea grew stronger. Beyond the Tinkertoy mashup of Jugend houses and high-rises, I saw another skyline, bristling with cruise vessels, tour boats, cranes, trawlers, vast container ships. The driver glanced back at me.

"Ever been to Finland before?"

"No."

"What do you think?" Before I could answer, we careened into a maze of narrow side streets. "A lot quieter here. Finns don't talk so much."

"I hadn't noticed."

"Oh, yeah. Know how you tell which Finn's the extrovert? He's the one staring at someone *else's* shoes. Here you are."

The car halted abruptly in front of a three-story house. A mid-century take on Jugend style, reinforced white concrete with carefully chosen Art Nouveau details—cedar shakes on the roof, small square windows, a hammered bronze door. A neatly laid-out garden, now all rattling stalks and desiccated leaves. The place didn't scream "rich fashion photographer" at the viewer: It was more like a polite nod before you were shown the way out.

Lindblad handed me a card.

W. Lindblad
HELSINGIN TAKSI 24 HOURS
9-363-9714

I stuck it in my pocket, paid the fare, and hopped out before the Audi disappeared in a haze of exhaust. I stood and tried to get my bearings. The Vicodin's fuzzy glow had faded hours ago. I raked a hand through my hair and wished I'd had a shower or some coffee, and started to dig around in my satchel for the Focalin when a harsh croaking echoed through the empty street. I looked up and saw a huge crow, the biggest I'd ever seen, perched on a narrow sill above the front door. It cocked its head and stared at me, clacked its beak, then made a strangled sound.

"*Hyvää iltaa.*"

Startled, I dropped my bag. The bronze door swung open, and a tall man in a faded work shirt and white cargo pants stepped out.

"Are you Cassandra?"

I nodded. The bird hopped from its perch onto the man's shoulder as I stammered, "That crow talks."

The man tossed something into the patch of skeletal plants. The bird flapped over and began to search among the dead leaves, clacking softly. The man said, "He's a raven. Apu. Short for 'thief.' Come inside."

I followed him into a living room where nearly everything was white—walls, ceiling, bleached hardwood floor. A mix of Saarinen and Ikea furniture; photos in simple black frames on the walls. Above the fireplace hung an oversize Jenny Saville painting of an emaciated runway model in a beaded gown that had been torn to shreds.

"Ilkka Kaltunnen." The tall man extended his hand. He was in his late thirties, with close-cropped brown hair, gray-flecked, and a lean face that might have been handsome if he ever smiled. Small, deep-set black eyes behind wire-rimmed glasses; skin so pale his face looked like it had been chipped from milky ice. He smelled of expensive cologne, vetiver and fig, and wood smoke. "Would you like some coffee?"

"Yeah. That would be great."

"Please." He gestured at a chair. "I'll be right back."

I couldn't bring myself to sit: The room felt like a set from *THX 1138*. Instead I dropped my bag and checked out the photos. A black-and-white homage to an Eadweard Muybridge stop-motion sequence, it featured a corpse posed upright, arms and legs extended as though in motion. In each photo the body was in a more advanced state of decay, until nothing remained but a skeleton. There was also a beautiful archival photo of a girl's mummified body. She was blindfolded, a broken spear in the crook of one slender arm, and what remained of her long blond hair was coiled around her neck.

"That's the Windeby Boy." I turned to see Ilkka, accompanied by a black-haired young woman in loose white trousers and a black T-shirt. "The Windeby Girl, they thought, but when they did DNA testing they learned it was a fourteen-year-old boy. He is one of the bog people from Schleswig-Holstein, they found him weighted down by logs and a great stone. A sacrifice. And this is my assistant, Suri."

The young woman smiled. She had broad shoulders, muscular arms that looked as though they could get you in a hammerlock, and surprisingly small hands, the nails squared off and lacquered indigo.

"Nice to meet you," she said. She set down a tray laden with pastries and poured our coffee, flashed me another smile, and left.

I settled cautiously into a chair with a mug, wondering if guests who spilled coffee in the white room ended up as dead photo subjects. I inclined my head toward the picture sequence. "Charles-François Jeandel?"

"Yes. They have never been published or exhibited. Except here, of course." He sank onto the couch across from me. "I have always heard this, but it's true: You have a remarkably good eye."

"It's better when I get a good night's sleep."

"Of course. Where are you staying?"

I frowned. Somewhere in the back of my mind I must have assumed it would be here. Before I could reply, Ilkka added, "Before I forget—a courier left this for you, early this morning."

He handed me a thick white envelope. No name or return address. I muttered thanks and stuck it in my bag.

Ilkka wasn't much for small talk. We sat in silence and drank our coffee. I ate one of the pastries and did my best to keep raspberry jam from oozing onto the pristine upholstery. From outside I heard a low croaking, and a moment later the raven hopped onto the windowsill and tapped its beak against the glass.

Ilkka stood and went to stare at the raven. He said something I couldn't understand, rapping his knuckles on the pane. The bird flew off.

"Did you train it to talk?"

"No." He smiled, showing very white teeth. "But I encouraged it."

"What does it say?"

"*Hyvää iltaa*. 'Good evening.' It will say that till spring. Then it will say *hyvää huomenta*."

"Meaning?"

" 'Good morning.' "

"How does it know the difference?"

"When the nights are eighteen hours long, everyone knows the difference."

We sat for a few minutes in silence. Ilkka continued to stare at the window. It was an effort to keep my hands from shaking. Finally I asked where the bathroom was, and Ilkka pointed down the hall.

"That way, on the left. If you reach the kitchen you've gone too far."

I mumbled thanks, retrieved my bag, and stumbled into the hall.

The arctic color scheme extended throughout the house. Alcoves held delicately carved bone figurines, a whale's tooth etched with a scene of a beheading. Some fashionably transgressive work by Deborah Turbeville, as well as more macabre photos, including a nineteenth-century cyanotype of a string quartet of skeletons in evening dress, and images from an archeological dig—piles of human skulls, skeletons missing skulls or limbs.

Other than the Turbevilles, none of them reflected the sort of blingy taste I associated with the fashion photographers I'd known, especially those who'd made their money in the Go-Go '90s. I didn't recognize any of Ilkka's own work on the walls. There was no indication he'd ever done commercial photography, except for that Jenny Saville deconstruction of a couture model. It all seemed coldly ascetic, almost monastic, save for the faint scent of wood smoke and vetiver. I passed an office where Suri sat staring at a laptop, and finally reached the bathroom.

I locked the door, took a long pull at the Jack Daniel's, and checked out the medicine cabinet. Nothing but soaps wrapped in black tissue, the same autumnal scent as Ilkka's cologne. I stuck one in my bag, washed my face, and exchanged my frayed turtleneck for my striped shirt; popped a couple of Focalin and opened the envelope Ilkka had given me. Inside was a vinyl wallet containing three thousand euros. Anton had kept his side of the deal. I counted out half the notes and slipped them into my own tattered wallet, shoved the rest into my pocket, and returned to the living room.

Ilkka stood by the window, talking on a cell phone. He shot me an apologetic look, spoke for another minute, and signed off.

"Sorry. That was my wife; one of our children is not feeling well at school. She may come back early with him if the nurse thinks he should come home."

"You've got kids?" I could no more imagine children here than in my own apartment.

"Two. A boy and a girl." He gazed at the frozen garden, then turned and gestured toward the hall. "Come. I'll show you what you've come to see. Tell me, how do you know Anton?"

"I don't. He asked me to look at some photos he's interested in buying. Yours. I never heard of him before two days ago."

"You might want to keep it that way."

"Why?"

"We have a saying: *Kun paholaiselle antaa pikkusormen, se perkele vie koko käden.* 'If you give your little finger to the Devil, it will take your whole hand.'"

We turned down a passageway, and he continued. "I was delighted when Anton told me he had retained you to authenticate my photos. *Dead Girls* was a very important book for me; I found it in a used bookstore when I was at university. I hadn't realized there were other people doing the kind of photography that I wanted to do. I felt as though I suddenly had permission to create my own work. All those photos of yours, they aged well. Better than your punks did."

He gave a barking laugh. "Iggy Pop and Johnny Rotten, dinosaurs selling insurance and butter on TV. So much for anarchy. And I saw your *Stern* photograph online, the Kamestos death mask. Everything has a price, yes?"

"I don't care who's buying the round, long as he pays."

"I hope Anton has paid you well, then. He can afford to."

I shrugged. The truth was, I was caught off guard by the fact that both Anton and Ilkka knew my work. I'd spent thirty years living under the world's radar, scraping by on booze and whatever drugs I could scrounge from Phil Cohen. It was unsettling to think I had a second life, courtesy of some old black-and-white photos of dead people. Ilkka looked at me curiously.

"You're a cult figure," he said. "Didn't you know that?"

"Must be a very small cult."

"It is," said Ilkka, and laughed.

The hall ended in a room with wood-paneled walls and a staircase. Ilkka stopped me before I could start upstairs. "Not that way. Here—"

He slid aside a panel to reveal an alarm box, punched in a code, and slid open a section of wall. Last time I'd heard of something like this was in a Nancy Drew book. Ilkka stepped inside. He switched on a light and beckoned me to follow, closing the door behind us.

"Watch your head." He ducked down a narrow flight of stairs. "This was the original servants' quarters: The kitchen and pantry were down here. I had it made into my darkroom."

I followed him until we reached the bottom. Ilkka held the door for me and bowed. "Welcome to Valhalla," he said.

7

There's an old Van Halen album cover, a detail from a painting by an artist who went insane. The painting shows a cross section of his skull, compartments filled with gruesome Freudian nightmares and traumas—fleshless limbs, beatings, hobnailed boots.

Ilkka's house was like that. Upstairs was the tightly wound superego; the darkroom was like entering his reptilian forebrain. A faint, familiar smell filled the place—the vinegary scent of acetic acid; liquid gum arabic and ammonia; sulfur dioxide, silver intensifiers—chemicals used for film processing. There was an underlying odor of drains. Photos from Ilkka's fashion spreads covered the walls: Haute couture models attacking each other with scissors; an ebony-skinned woman with a banana-yellow tree frog on her tongue; a girl slumped on a toilet seat, billows of white tulle obscuring her torso.

All shared the extrasolar flare that had been Ilkka's

trademark—miniature novas blooming from eyes or scissors or a drop of water on a girl's bare back. There were also a few pictures of heavy-metal bands, and some grainy black-and-white crime-scene photos. "That's how I got started." Ilkka indicated a newspaper clipping of a corpse stuffed in the trunk of a Volvo. "I was at university in Jyväskylä, doing art history, and the police needed someone to take photos for them. Their regular guy went on vacation to Ibiza, so I filled in for him. Then he never came back. I loved it."

"Why'd you quit?"

"I didn't want to stay in Jyväskylä. I decided to study archaeology, so I moved to Oslo and took some classes at university. That's where I met Anton; I used to hang out at his club. He introduced me to Jürgen Borne—you know his work, right? Jürgen was looking for an assistant, and he hired me. I worked on that *Vogue Italia* spread, the one with Chira Hendrix and the reindeer. That was my idea. After that, it all came together."

I peered at another newspaper photo—a kitchen with a woman curled on the linoleum, hands clutched protectively around her head. There was a hammer beside her, blond hair caught between its claws. Droplets of blood glowed like liquid mercury spilled across the floor. He'd found his gift early on.

"I still have it set up for film." Ilkka flicked on more lights. "But mostly I do digital now."

Cabinets and shelves lined the walls, crammed with boxes and camera equipment. The enameled sink had been divided into sections for agitating and developing film. Photos and contact sheets were strewn across a counter beside a flat-screen monitor. There was a large table in the center of the room, and an old map chest was shoved into a corner.

"I know." Ilkka grinned. "It's a mess."

"No, it's great. It looks—" I started to say, *It looks human.* "It looks like a good place to work."

"Oh, it is. My wife hates it: She doesn't want the children to see my pictures. One reason for all the locks. She hasn't been down here since I built it. No one has, except for me. And now you."

He began to clear the table, moving glassine envelopes and contact sheets and finally a large camera with an old-fashioned flashbulb attachment.

"That a Speed Graphic?"

Ilkka cradled the rig against his chest. "Yes. My baby."

"Can I see it?"

He hesitated before handing it to me. "Be very careful."

I was. The Speed Graphic's the camera you see in old movies, toted by newspapermen at crime scenes, political campaigns, behind enemy lines during the war. Weegee had one. It's an amazing rig—three viewfinders, two shutters, everything operated manually.

You had to be fast to use a Speed Graphic. It helped to have Weegee's supernatural gift for knowing when to push the shutter release, a microsecond before your moment disappeared. He once said, "With a camera like that the cops will assume that you belong on the scene and will let you get behind police lines."

I held it gingerly, a nice weight. Silken black finish, chrome trim. The chrome marked it as a prewar model, and I looked at Ilkka curiously. "How long have you had this?"

"I bought it at a pawn shop in Jyväskylä. That's how I got the police job: I looked the part."

The camera even had its original flash attachment, a concave seven-inch reflector with a bulb still attached—an old General Electric Synchro-Flash, blue-coated, which meant it was used for color and not black and white. Those old bulbs were intensely bright, five hundred thousand lumens released over a fraction of a second.

"You have trouble finding bulbs for this?"

He smiled ruefully. "Yes. For a long time I had a stockpile, but they're getting harder to find, even on eBay. That's the last one until I find a new source."

I handed it back to him with great care. He set it in a cabinet and retrieved a white cloth.

"I don't know how much time you'll need for this." He began to clean the table's surface. "But Anton is extremely controlling. He needs things to be perfect, orderly. In this case, no doubts about authenticity. You understand?"

"Yeah, sure. But you've worked with him before, right? He owns some of your work. That's what I assumed, anyway."

"Yes, he has some of my work." Ilkka's tone grew terse. "Old police pictures that I sold him when I was young and needed the money. But nothing from this sequence. No one has ever seen any of these."

"Not even Suri? Or your wife?"

He shook his head. "I set up a temporary link to one of the images. You saw that?"

"The guy with the window smashed against his face?"

"Yes. Gluggagægir."

He tossed the cloth into a sink, rummaged in a drawer for two pairs of white cotton gloves. He gave a pair to me and pulled his on, waiting as I did the same. Then he crossed to the map chest, withdrew a key, and unlocked the bottom drawer. With great care he removed a large print, roughly 44 × 28, covered with protective tissue paper. He set it on the table and painstakingly removed the protective tissue. I whistled softly.

It was the image Anton had shown me online: the black-haired guy in that incongruously bright, blood-striped parka, his broken face shrouded by splintered wood and shards of glass.

But there was no comparison between the on-screen image and the real thing. It was printed on super glossy paper, probably Crystal Archive, with saturated color so intense it was as though I stood in the photographer's shoes with the boy's corpse at my feet. Beneath a moonless sky, snow glittered blindingly from black spars of rock. A drop of blood on the shattered windowpane looked as though it would stain my finger if I touched it. Where the jagged spear of glass pierced the boy's cheek, Ilkka's trademark flare shone so brilliantly that I blinked.

"It's incredible. But, Jesus. What happened?"

"As you see. He is dead. This was in Vemdalen, Sweden, near the border with Norway. December 1991." He ticked off the information as though reading a train schedule. "Gluggagægir is one of the Jólasveinar. The Yuleboys."

"The Yuleboys? That's a cult?"

Ilkka looked startled. "No," he said quickly. "A folktale, a Christmas legend used to scare children into being good. The Jólasveinar are trolls. The original legends were quite frightening. Now they're utterly commercialized, like the Smurfs—cartoons to sell Christmas cards and toys. Like everything else in our heritage, they have been corrupted by Christianity and capitalism."

"They're Finnish?"

He shook his head. "No. I mean our shared northern culture. Finns are not Scandinavian, but we are Nordic. And the Jólasveinar are Icelandic. But Iceland was settled by the Vikings, so their origins were Norse, and the Jólasveinar tradition is even more ancient than that. I have researched it for many years, and even I don't know how ancient—thousands of years, at least. Over time the myth was degraded to accommodate Christian beliefs. Here in Finland, it was even worse: We have no record of our own true history.

"The Kalevala is nothing but stories cobbled together by a single man a hundred and sixty years ago," he said with disdain. "Stories of men and witches and little gods—but our gods are not the true gods. For that we must look to an older world where the ancient ways remain alive."

"Like Norway?"

"Yes. And Iceland, which is where our purest Nordic culture survived. That is what I believe. Originally there were many Jólasveinar, but manufacturers have chosen only thirteen, the ones who might sell the most toys. The Jólasveinar go creeping around your house in the thirteen days before Christmas, and one visits each night. Gluggagægir is the Peeper: He spies in windows. Then there's Hurðaskellir, Door Slammer; and þvörusleikir, Spoon Licker; Lampaskuggi, Lamp Shadow; and Ketrókur, Meat Hook, and—"

"What, no geese a-laying?" I laughed. "Meat Hook—there's a Hallmark moment if I ever saw one."

"No, the Jólasveinar are not nice like Christmas elves; they

47

never became that Christian."

I turned back to the photo. "So did they catch the guy who did this?"

"Never. None of the bodies was ever discovered, by the police or anyone else, as far as I know." He lifted his head to stare at me with those icy gray eyes. "I do not mean that I was the murderer. I was not."

He returned to the map chest for another photo, set it down beside the first, and peeled back the white tissue. "This is Spoon Licker."

I grimaced.

"I know," Ilkka said softly. "Horrible."

But his gaze remained fixed on the print, his mouth parted as though he stared at something unspeakably lovely. I could see why.

An old man lay in a snowbank, head turned to the camera. He wore a stained blue sweatshirt, sneakers held together with duct tape, faded cotton pants that looked like hospital scrubs. One eye was open, milky blue clotted with red. Where the other eye had been was a hole, with a pointillist spray of crimson on the snow behind him. A metal spoon had been thrust between his gaping jaws. His tongue was gone, and Ilkka's signature radiance flared from the spoon like a lit fuse. It was like a scene from some terrible fairy tale: the witch forced to wear red-hot iron shoes, the prince whose eyes are scratched out by thorns.

Yet it was also stunningly beautiful. Ilkka had captured veins of blue within the snow, and the spray of blood might have been feathers or petals. I searched in vain for footprints, evidence of a killer or onlookers.

"How did you know?" I asked. "Who tipped you off?"

"How did Weegee know? I have sharp ears. And eyes."

"But the police must have suspected you."

"I told you, no one ever knew of these deaths or cared. I did not know this man. Look at him." He jabbed a finger at the print. "This carcass—who was he? I will tell you: he was nothing. *Kulkuri*—a 'tramp.' If his life had been worth something, someone would have searched for him! Someone would have mourned him. No one did. There was no search party, no investigation. Winters are very long in this part of the world. By spring, he was gone. They were all gone."

"Gone?"

"Wolves and bears, lynx. Ravens." He gestured dismissively. "Winter swallows everything."

"But winter didn't kill him. Or wolves."

"Neither did I."

"But you know who did."

"'Death will claim no man until his time has come, and nothing will save a man who is fated to die. Therefore be bold: to die in fear is the worst death of all.' That is what the sagas teach us, and I would not argue with those words." His gaze remained unfathomable. "I'll show you the rest."

One by one he set out the remaining photos, his gloved hands meticulously removing each sheet of the protective tissue until the entire sequence covered the table. All were in the same oversize color format; all had been shot in the winter; all had, somewhere, Ilkka's signature flare.

"This is Svellabrjótur. Icebreaker."

Beneath the ice of some northern lake, air pockets and bubbles formed a glittering constellation in a man's blond hair. His eyes bulged, and his mouth opened as though caught in the middle of a yawn. The photo had been taken at night with a long exposure, beneath a moon so brilliant it resembled a halogen bulb in a sky streaked with stars. It would have taken a while to set up, and then the photographer would have been there in the frozen dark with a corpse beneath the ice, calmly counting the minutes till he closed the aperture. I wondered how much the temperature dropped when Ilkka entered a room.

Ketrókur, Meat Hook, seemed almost mundane compared to the other pictures. A middle-aged man, heavyset and wearing a black overcoat and a business suit, sprawled on a rocky, snow-sifted beach with a meat hook through his head.

"Where was this?"

"Huk Beach, in Oslo. A nude beach."

"It looks cold for a nude beach."

"Homosexuals would go there for sex. He was not mourned, either." He gestured at the final photograph. "Hurðaskellir. Door Slammer."

A landscape so heavily drifted with snow that there was no sense of scale: Fir trees, boulders—all had disappeared beneath blue-white dunes poised to break above a calcified sea. The shutter speed was so fast that I picked out individual snowflakes as they swept near the lens in crystalline explosions. Elsewhere, whirling snow made it seem as though you looked at the scene through gauze, streaked black where the wind exposed a bare tree limb.

But no matter where you looked—no matter that the sky was lowering and featureless—that unearthly radiance suffused everything, as though the world had erupted into a ghostly supernova. It was the kind of photograph that makes a career; a once-in-a-lifetime shot.

And if Ilkka was telling the truth, no one else had ever seen it. I was so entranced that it took a minute for me to notice the body. It lay in the foreground on a plank—a door—outstretched limbs so pale I'd mistaken them for ridges of snow. Unlike the other corpses, this one was a naked woman, small breasted, with platinum hair. Her face was bleached of color, her lips leaden; her open eyes revealed irises cloudy green like old glass. Her head was turned so that she gazed directly at the camera. Her body was eerily untouched by snow. I stared at her, my neck prickling, and fought an almost irresistible urge to disappear into that brutal, beautiful space.

"They do not sicken you," murmured Ilkka.

"No. They're incredible."

"Most people would find them horrifying."

I shrugged. Photography is the art that justifies atrocity: war photography, pornography, memento mori, footprints left on a landscape where the last great auk died. None of us is innocent.

"The way you capture light . . ." I stared at the girl's unseeing eyes, a travesty of the detached gaze all great photographers cultivate. "I've never seen anything like it. You didn't use a flash gun?"

"No—that would have been *petkuttaa*, a 'cheat.' Only the flashbulb. I show what the world hides from us—the true world. The sun doesn't lie. The night doesn't lie."

"But how did you do it? It's impossible. There's no available light."

"No. What is impossible is to take a photograph where there is only light. You can never shoot the midday sun without a filter; you know that. But there is no true darkness. There is always light, somewhere."

"Not enough for that." I gestured at the print. "Not enough to make everything look fucking incandescent."

"There is always light," repeated Ilkka. "Buried beneath the earth, even. Not everyone can see it. But I do." He leaned forward, scrutinizing me. "Just as you see something else. It is there...."

Hs finger hovered alongside my right eye, the raw scar that had not yet healed. "A flaw behind your retina. I can see that, too. Odin traded one eye for wisdom and the gift of true sight. Perhaps you have done the same, yes?"

He drew back, and we gazed at the photos.

"All these people," I said. "Did you see some flaw in them?"

"I know nothing about any of them, except what I have told you. But they deserved to die. They were unclean: Their own darkness had invaded them. Whatever light they possess now, it came from me."

"Is this it?" I stared at the table. "Just these five?"

"Isn't that enough?"

"Anton told me there were six."

Ilkka remained silent. I stared at his chiseled face and ice-gray eyes, trying to make sense of all this. I caught no chemical whiff of fear or adrenaline, nothing to signal that he'd touched any weapon other than a shutter release. He might be crazy, but he was telling the truth.

Part of it, anyway. Ilkka Kaltunnen might be lying about that sixth photo, but he wasn't the murderer. Someone else was. Anton? In which case Ilkka was blackmailing him, despite the fact that Ilkka was inextricably bound to whatever had happened out there in the snow, beneath the ice. Not just complicit in any cover-up or failure to report the murders, but in whatever bizarre belief system had left at least five people murdered, their deaths unnoticed and unmourned.

I'd never heard of a murderer who kept a court photographer, but there's always a first time. Ilkka either witnessed each killing or he was tipped off before the blood cooled. He got his money shot and split.

And money definitely would be an object. Large-format images like these cost a bundle to produce. No commercial lab would have developed or printed them without asking questions or calling the cops.

Photographers are like professional stage magicians. They admire each other's work and share tips but seldom reveal exactly how the trick was done. I figured I'd give it a shot. "How'd you process them?"

Ilkka pointed to an adjoining room. I walked in and found a huge machine, sleek and white as a plastic coffin beneath a translucent plastic tarp—a first-generation Chromira LED printer. He must have socked away a small fortune to pay for it: In the '90s, this rig would have set you back fifty grand plus change.

But it would also allow you to produce your own prints in-house, with no embarrassing inquiries about blood on the snow. I saw another door at the end of the room, with half a dozen light switches beside it. I was willing to bet that was where the big color negs were processed, in an equally expensive rig.

Yet as far as I could see, the only thing Ilkka had ever used it for was a sequence that produced just five photos. Where was the sixth photo that Anton had referred to? Ilkka had told me he mostly shot in digital now, and there was no sign of any other oversize prints, unless he stored them in the map chest. What photographer invests a hundred grand in equipment he hardly uses?

A rich, obsessive control freak locked into some crazy-ass death cult. He and Anton deserved each other. I returned to the table, where Ilkka gazed transfixed at his own work. "It's good, isn't it, Cassandra?"

"It's brilliant." I meant it. "I'd still like to know how you did that."

The overhead light candled the lenses of Ilkka's glasses as he smiled but said nothing.

"What if you and Anton can't agree on a price for these?" I asked. "You got other buyers lined up?"

"That's none of your business."

"So you're just selling him these prints and the negs?"

"There are no negs. I've destroyed them all. These are the only prints."

"You won't keep a set?"

Ilkka continued to stare at the table. "That time is gone," he said at last. "I am not sorry: There were a lot of evil things, and I do not need help remembering them. These will be the only prints."

It was a good strategy. Most photographers make money by selling multiple prints run from a negative or, these days, a digital image. But the priciest photos, the ones that go for the big bucks at auction or through private transactions—those are often old daguerreotypes or ambrotypes, images produced in a one-off format, because that was pretty much the only game in town, back in the nineteenth century. Destroying original negs creates the kind of artificial scarcity that keeps the art world in business.

It would be possible to duplicate Ilkka's pictures, of course, if you could get your hands on them. Still, to get anything approaching the quality of these originals would be almost impossible, and someone with a good eye—me, for instance—would recognize the difference between a first-generation print and one made from a copy neg.

That's leaving out the law-enforcement issues that would emerge if these images ever hit the Internet. Whatever he'd been like in the winter of 1991, these days Ilkka didn't seem like a guy who'd want to chance scandal and possible prison time. I wondered how much he was asking for the sequence.

And I wondered why he was selling it now.

Ilkka's cell phone chimed. He answered it and walked into the room with the Chromira printer, talking quietly in Finnish. When he was gone, I quickly stepped to the map chest and slid open the top drawer, looking for a sixth print. It was empty. So was the next drawer and all the rest. Unless he had extra copies stashed elsewhere, those five prints were it. I did a swift reconnoiter of the room but didn't see anyplace he might have stored them flat. Rolled up, they might have been anywhere, but I doubted Ilkka would be so cavalier with his trophies.

I searched inside a few more drawers—nothing but old contact sheets and film paraphernalia—then wandered to a counter strewn with CDs by Can, Kraftwerk, Alan Hovhaness, along with a bunch of dour-looking Scandinavian composers I'd never heard of. The guy definitely suffered from Stockhausen Syndrome.

But there were some old cassette tapes, too, with handmade labels sporting xeroxed images of inverted crosses and guys in corpse-paint makeup, the band names scrawled in Magic Marker: Sarcófago, Celtic Frost, Viðar, Bathory. I was vaguely aware of Bathory, and I knew Viðar only because they were Scandinavian, and Ilkka had shot their first album cover.

I glanced at the Celtic Frost tapes, picked up one with the word *Blot* penciled on its cardboard insert. Ilkka was still occupied with his phone call, so I stuck it in my pocket, grabbing two more at random. I don't even own a cassette player, but what the hell. A minute later he walked back into the room.

"That was my wife. Oskari, our little boy, is feeling worse, I have to get him at school. She's in a meeting and can't leave."

He hurriedly covered the prints with their protective sheaths, replaced them in the map chest, and locked it. We both peeled off our white cotton gloves and retraced our steps back upstairs.

"I'm not sure how long this will take." His face looked drawn. "It's the flu. She worries every time Oskari gets a fever. If he's really sick, I may have to take him to the doctor."

He seemed more disturbed than I'd expect someone to be over a kid with a cold, but it was no skin off my nose. "That's okay. I think I've got enough to report back to Anton."

"If you have any questions, we can talk about it this evening at dinner. He will be anxious to finish the deal; you might even have the chance to meet him."

I shrugged. "Yeah, sure. Look, can I ask you one thing? How much are you asking for these?"

He named a figure that was double what I would have imagined.

Anton was willing to pay 1990s art-world money, considerably adjusted for inflation. "A cash transaction," Ilkka added.

Again, I kicked myself for not demanding more money from Anton.

We reached the main floor with its long white corridor like a tunnel in a dream. The handwoven rugs muffled our footsteps. Downstairs, surrounded by the familiar clutter of camera equipment, I'd almost forgotten where I was.

Now I felt unpleasantly aware that I was in a foreign land where I knew no one, trapped in a silent house where photos of the dead radiated power, and the living drifted side by side without speaking.

Finally we reached his office. Ilkka spoke to Suri, and I waited in the hall until he returned.

"Suri will help you find something for lunch," he said. "I'll let her know when I expect to be back for dinner and if Anton will join us. We can talk more then. I am looking forward to it."

Unexpectedly, Ilkka rested his hand upon my shoulder. For an instant I saw my own face reflected in his wire-rimmed glasses. "Thank you, Cassandra. It is easier for me to let them go, knowing that you have seen them. It is our gaze that keeps them alive. But it is terrible, sometimes, to have that as a gift."

He squeezed my arm and left.

8

"Come in, please." Suri smiled and waved me into Ilkka's office. "It'll take me just a minute to finish up, then we can get something to eat."

I looked around while she fiddled with her computer. Wooden filing cabinets covered one wall, beneath framed copies of magazine covers and pictures of Ilkka with people like Isabella Blow and Franca Sozzani. Covers from *Vogue Italia, Elle, Women's Wear Daily;* plaques for the Iconique Societas Award and Kontakt Award. A painted antique cupboard held odd ephemera on its upper shelves, high enough that small children couldn't reach them: old pop-up books showing Red Riding Hood being swallowed by the wolf; hand-colored pictures of Bluebeard from a Victorian toy theater. A fragile copy of *Der Struwwelpeter* opened to a lurid illustration of a girl in flames. Had this guy ever seen the Disney version of anything?

I picked up a stack of vintage postcards—some sort of macabre Christmas cards, dating to the late nineteenth or early twentieth century. Every one featured a leering devil doing something unpleasant to a child—stuffing a boy into a burlap sack, brandishing a handful of sticks at a shrieking girl. In some pictures, the devil's feet were cloven; in others he wore stylish shoes or hobnailed boots. Saint Nicholas accompanied him in a few images, but more often the devil cavorted alone. The same greeting was printed on every card. Gruss vom Krampus! I fanned them out as though they were a fortune-telling deck.

"What are these?"

"Ah, you found Ilkka's collection." Suri laughed. "Those are old Krampus cards. He buys them on eBay."

I held up a picture of a devil riding a broomstick, his long tongue coiled suggestively. "But what *is* that?"

"You don't know Krampus? He travels with St. Nicholas and beats bad children. You know, to make them behave." She laughed again. "I think it must have worked; he's very scary."

"Finland must have a lot of traumatized kids."

"Oh, he's not Finnish. German—no, Austrian. Maybe both. Here we have Father Christmas with his reindeer because, you know, this is where he lives, on Korvatunturi Mountain in Lapland. The Finns invented Father Christmas—all of it, with the reindeer and the little elves and the snow."

I pointed at the cards. "But not this?"

"No, not Krampus. That is Ilkka's taste."

"It's a little strange."

"Ilkka is interested in old things, especially rituals about the dead."

"Like the bog boy?"

"Yes. And Pyhäinpäivä, what we used to call Kekri—All Saints'

Day—the end of harvest, before winter comes. People would visit the cemeteries, because that is when the dead come back. I don't know why he likes to study these things, but he does. Old religions, old legends. I'll shut down now. I'm hungry."

She turned, and I noticed a framed photo in one corner of the desk: Ilkka and a beautiful blond woman on the deck of a sailboat, their arms around two young children. A towheaded girl, barely a toddler, and a boy a few years older. He was completely bald, with his father's thin mouth and narrow eyes. No eyebrows or eyelashes. I thought of the mummified boy in the Windeby bog.

"That's Oskari," said Suri in a soft voice. She picked up the picture and studied it. "Their son. He has a very rare cancer, leukemia that goes to the brain. He was in remission, but a few months ago it came back. The care here is very good, but he is not responding to it anymore. That's why Ilkka is so upset when he gets sick. They want to take him overseas for an experimental treatment, but it's very expensive."

"I bet."

His son's cancer treatment might explain Ilkka's decision to sell the Yuleboy photos. Or maybe something else was going on and this was just a good excuse to finally unload them. Either way, I decided I'd give a big thumbs-up to Bredahl, maybe even invent another interested party to jack up the price.

We walked to the front door. Suri stopped to retrieve a pair of boots, then tugged a brightly knitted cap over her hair. "Have you seen any of the city yet? No? We can walk down to the harbor market. If you don't mind walking."

"Nah, I don't mind."

I grabbed my leather jacket and followed her outside. What I really wanted was a drink, but I didn't feel like pulling out my private stash of whiskey in front of this girl. We were almost to the sidewalk when there was a noise behind us, a sound like tumbling dice. I looked back to see the raven perched on the lintel, clacking its beak as it stared at me with one baleful yellow eye.

"*Hyvää iltaa,*" it croaked, and flew above the barren treetops.

9

Gray haze clouded the air as we walked to the harbor. It took me a few minutes to realize this wasn't fog or pollution, but the light, or lack of it. Everything looked dingy and slightly out of focus, like staring at the world through a dirty window screen. Suri walked briskly beside me, head down against the wind. "Why haven't you visited the harbor?"

"I just got here. I took a cab from the train station straight to Ilkka's place."

"You could have walked. I hope the taxi driver didn't charge you much."

The streets were surprisingly crowded for such a miserable day, though for all I knew, this qualified as balmy weather in Finland. No one met my eyes. The Finns seemed far more animated when talking on their cell phones than to one another. Suri wore fingerless gloves that enabled her to text faster than I thought humanly possible. It made me feel even more adrift in a sunless dream, surrounded by ghosts that didn't know they were dead. The only sounds were the slapping of waves against the docks and the shriek of gulls wheeling overhead.

"Do you eat meat?" Suri stopped texting long enough to glance at me, and I nodded. "Excellent. There's a good hot dog kiosk here."

We walked to a small cart beneath a faded awning. The hot dog was good. I hadn't realized how famished I was—I hadn't eaten for almost two days. I wolfed it down along with a Jaffa soda and got another, heaped with onions. I needed some vegetables.

"It's good, isn't it?" Suri held her hot dog delicately, then took a bite.

"It's great." I looked around in vain for a napkin, finally wiped my greasy hands on my jacket. "What would be even greater is if there was someplace we could get a drink."

"Yeah, sure." She gestured to where people milled in front of a brightly lit entryway. "We'll go there, if you like."

"How about someplace not so touristy?"

"But you are a tourist." She smiled. "Yeah, I know a place. It takes a few minutes, but it's nice to walk outside."

That was questionable. I tried to reconfigure my scarf so my ears didn't freeze, and hurried to keep up with her. "How long you been working for Ilkka?"

"As his assistant? About ten years, since I was twenty. Before that I was one of his models. He worked with me since I was fourteen, then when I got too old, he hired me to help him on shoots. Now I mostly just do office work."

"Were you in any of the famous pictures?"

"Several. The one for *Vogue Italia* with the reindeer—that was my first big job, up in Lapland. I froze my ass off. But I didn't get sick. Some of the other girls did, but they weren't Finns."

"Were you involved with him?"

"Ilkka? No. He never went with the girls. His wife, Kati—she's very beautiful. And he loves his children. Even back then, before he was married, he was always about work. He loves very cold places, and I don't think too many models wanted to spend time on the ice in Lapland. So he used me a lot."

"In his music videos? Were you in those?"

Suri made a face. "Ugh! No, never! Those people scared me. Ilkka hung out with them for a while, but once he met Kati he stopped."

"You mean the Oslo club scene?"

"I don't know." She hesitated. "Well, okay, yes. All that black metal—he used to play it when we were shooting. I hated it. That was a very bad time; bad things happened to people then." She took in my leather jacket and steel-tipped boots, the scar beside my eye. "But maybe you like that."

I started to frame another question, but she shook her head vehemently. "*Ei.* It's bad luck to talk of the Devil. Here, this way..."

We turned onto a narrow road. Nothing that would appeal to anyone just off a Nordic cruise ship—buildings with steel mesh in the windows, empty containers that reeked of gasoline. From the loading dock of a fish processing plant came a smell so foul I held my breath till we passed it.

Suri walked lightly, glossy hair streaming from beneath her cap. At the end of the street we turned into an alley where a neon sign washed the pavement an ugly, blistered pink. A ratty-looking mongrel was tied to a pole beside the door of a corrugated shack. It was the last place I'd expect someone like Suri to hang out, but she walked straight past the dog and went inside.

The place was dim and smelled of spilled beer and fried fish. Several men sat drinking in a cloud of smoke, despite warning signs that showed a cigarette with a red X through it. Behind the bar, a woman greeted Suri. She was even taller than I was, and built like a set of Marshall stacks.

Suri turned to me. "Beer okay?"

I nodded and found a table against the far wall. Suri joined me and set down two brimming glasses.

"I'll have to get back soon," she said. "Ilkka left me some paperwork."

My beer tasted as though it had been salted. The men turned to stare at us; at Suri, actually. As she removed her parka and knit cap and shook her hair out, the grimy bar suddenly looked like the louche backdrop for a fashion shoot.

"*Kippis*—cheers." Suri lifted her glass to me and made an impressive dent in her beer. "How do you know Ilkka? Are you old friends?"

"I wouldn't call us that."

"He took you into his workroom downstairs. His *temppeli*, his 'sanctum'—that's what I call it. I've known him all these years, but he's never let me see it. He doesn't even allow Kati down there. So I thought the two of you must be very close."

"We have a mutual friend. Well, a mutual acquaintance, anyway. Guy named Anton Bredahl."

"Ugh." Suri grimaced. "You know him?"

"We've never actually met, just talked online. Why?"

"He's creepy. He was into death metal, then black metal. Mayhem and Viðar and Darkthrone, bands like that. He had a club in Oslo; I went twice with Ilkka. I hated it. I couldn't hear for two days. The people there freaked me out. He had a bouncer at that club, really scary guy." She shuddered.

"All bouncers are scary. That's what they pay them for."

"Not like this one." She lowered her voice and leaned across the table. "He cut people up—dead people, people Anton had killed for business. There was a girl, a prostitute from Estonia; she disappeared. And another guy, too, a drug dealer. This guy took the bodies and cut them up and buried the pieces. Someone I know saw him, he was with his girlfriend one night; she was carrying a bag, and there was a head in it."

I laughed. "A head? How'd they know it was a head if it was in a bag?"

Suri stared moodily at her beer. "I don't like to talk about those people."

"Like Anton?"

"Like I said—creepy."

"Old creepy or young creepy?"

"Not that old. Ilkka's age. He lived for a while in Berlin and sold black-market stuff, before the Wall came down. Then he came back to Oslo and started Forsvar—his club. All the dark metal bands play there. He has a back room where they hang out, a private room."

"Did you go into it?"

"No. Ilkka did, but he told me I wouldn't like it." She rubbed her arms, shivering. "Those guys were into bad stuff."

"Drugs?"

"Yes, drugs, though mostly they liked beer. But there were other things. Anton is *kiero*—'warped.' He collects photos of dead people."

"Well, there're photographers like that; lots of people collect their work. They get a ton of money for shooting dead people."

"Yes, I know that kind of stuff. But that's not what I mean. Anton buys pictures by murderers, also drawings and paintings. American murderers, some Germans, Indonesian, whatever he can find. Serial killers."

"You mean like John Wayne Gacy? Those clown paintings? What an idiot. They were terrible."

"Some people don't think so. Musicians in some of those bands, they collect them. Anton sells them photos, and other things. Anton collects these things himself, and he knows people who would pay a lot of money for them. That's how Ilkka met him—Ilkka used to be a crime photographer, did you know? Before the Internet these collectors would meet at a hotel room in Berlin or New York or Oslo. Now they do business online."

"Or in Anton's club."

"That's why I didn't get too close. And you know, the head."

"You ever meet his customers?"

"I tried not to. But Ilkka never did much business like that," she added earnestly. "Sometimes he sells one of his old crime photos to Anton, as a favor. I have to make the arrangements. It's not illegal; you'd think it would be, but it's not. Murderabilia, it's called. Some people only collect from serial killers in jail. Some people, they like autographs or . . ."

She made a face, and went on. "Hair. Or fingernail clippings. All from murderers. I think it should be against the law."

That might explain how Anton found out about me. It also might explain the sudden spike in prices for *Dead Girls.* To a completist, maybe my passing association with a serial killer would be enough; the photo in *Stern* would lead them to my book and then, in Anton's case, to me.

I leaned across the table and covered Suri's delicate hands with my own. She smiled, and I drew her hand to my mouth, kissed one knuckle then let my tongue trace the cleft between two fingers, tasting salt and ink. After a moment she withdrew her hand, still smiling. My eyes lingered on the ring on her third finger, a thick band of silver set with a moonstone.

"My girlfriend," she said. "For Christmas. We're engaged."

"Too bad." I sank back into my chair. "I don't get it. You say you hate this, but you still work for Ilkka. Which means you have to deal with people like Anton."

Suri finished her beer. "Yes, I know. I'm a hypocrite. But selling crime photos, it's not so different from fashion photography. Bodies are just objects to them. Nobody cares if a girl weighs seven stone and a photographer makes her pretend to overdose and puts her in a Galliano dress. Why should someone care more about a dead body than one that's pretending to be dead?"

"But you posed for those shots with Ilkka. What, did he hold a gun to your head?"

"Do you know why he stopped doing fashion work?"

"He got married and had kids. Old story."

"He had to call Emergency 999 during a London session because a girl was so malnourished she almost died. That was when he stopped doing fashion work. That girl was me."

I looked at her arms, beautifully defined, her broad high cheekbones and strong square chin. "How much is seven stone?"

"Ninety-eight pounds. That's why I work with him. He saved my life."

I started to point out that he was also the guy who'd been photographing emaciated girls in the snow, but she cut me off.

"It was a brave thing, really. He doesn't make so much money now. Kati has a good job, but it's hard because of Oskari's treatments. They keep trying different things, and now they want to go to a clinic in Mexico. But it's very, very expensive. And they lost a lot of money in October—some bad investments. They had a bad money advisor, a real asshole. I hear Ilkka arguing on the phone with him all the time. I hope he can afford to keep me." She glanced at her cell phone. "We should get back."

"I think I'll hang out here for a while. I'm beat."

True enough. But I was also tired of the whole situation—far too complicated for something that had nothing to do with me except a paycheck. And Anton Bredahl sounded more and more like the kind of asshole who should have lost his money in the crash, had there been anything like justice in this world.

Instead he was making god knows how much, dealing in pictures that were the next best thing to snuff photos. I had no qualms about Ilkka's photos, which were beautiful and seemed in line with a guy who collected Christmas cards with Satan on them. But I was getting pretty sick of rich people.

Suri pulled on her coat. I thanked her for the beer, then asked to borrow her cell phone. She handed it to me. I found Anton's number in my pocket, walked to a corner, and called him. He answered immediately.

"Hi, Suri."

"It's Cass Neary. I checked out those photos for you."

"Really? That was fast."

"Yeah, well, there's only five. Didn't take long. He's got a whole Batcave downstairs. Nice darkroom. Or it was, before he switched to digital."

"But these aren't digital?" Anton's voice rose slightly.

"No, they're all color film stock. My guess is Fuji Crystal Archive, Super Glossy. He uses an antique Graflex Speed Graphic camera, 4×5 color negs. He has his own processor and printer, so he handled it all himself. Chromira printer, probably state of the art when he got it. Still gets the job done."

"You're so good, Cass. But there were only five?"

"Yeah. But they're beautiful—fucking incredible."

"You're certain about the number?"

"Maybe he had more, but I didn't see them. He didn't talk like there were more. Believe me—photos this good? Five is plenty. I'd kill to know how he did them."

"Probably best not to know." Anton laughed again. He sounded relieved. "Did he discuss money?"

"I didn't bring it up. He did mention someone else who was interested. A guy, from Oslo, maybe? Someone with very deep pockets."

There was such a long silence, I was afraid he'd hung up.

So much for little Oskari's miracle cure, I thought, then heard Anton's voice, decidedly colder.

"Ilkka and I have a deal; you might remind him of that. Tell him I'll be there tonight. How do you want the rest of your fee?"

"Mail it to me back in New York." I gave him the address. "A cashier's check."

"Good-bye, Cass."

The call ended. I joined Suri, now talking animatedly with the bartender, and returned her phone. She'd notice that I'd called Anton, but I'd be gone by then. I thanked her for the beer.

"No worries." She smiled. "You're sure you don't want to come back with me? Ilkka will want to talk more at dinner."

"Yeah. Not sure what I'll do." I'd been tempted to stick around and talk shop with Ilkka, but I had no desire to meet Anton, especially after I'd just inflated the value of Ilkka's photos. "Find somewhere to crash for a while, probably."

"Okay." Suri tilted her head toward the giantess behind the bar. "Ritva will take care of you if you need anything."

Suri kissed me on my cheek. I watched her go, sorry I hadn't pressed my luck harder, got another beer from Barzilla, and retreated to a corner table. More customers floated in, but no one paid any attention to me. Music crackled from a speaker, the theme from *The Dukes of Hazzard* in Finnish. I downed my beer, then poured a jolt of whiskey from my stash. My head hummed with static, alcohol, Focalin, jet lag, exhaustion, all compounded by the memory of the photos in Ilkka's basement. More than anything, I felt the dull, familiar ache of envy. Not for Ilkka's wealth or house or family, or even his art collection. I've lived without all that for my entire life. I'll die without it, too.

No. I envied him his obsession, whatever alchemy of desire and fear had fueled those photographs. You don't get pictures like that without being in love with your subject.

But what kind of passion would drive someone to travel alone, in the depths of winter, to remote places where you wouldn't just risk hypothermia but prison? His son's medical expenses wouldn't be enough; the murders had occurred years before the kid was born. Some sick, extraordinary vision hid behind those wire-rimmed glasses and taciturn demeanor. I recognized it because the same fire had consumed me once, so long ago it was like dredging up the memory of a story I'd heard from someone else.

Quinn.

Once upon a time, that name conjured an entire world, lost to me now. No one before or since has ever made me feel like that or see like that. Cigarette smoke and the blinding rush of amyl nitrate, the feverish rush of Quinn himself, sex and speed and the scratch of a needle on vinyl.

But it wasn't just sex. Even after he disappeared, the enduring sense that Quinn was out there somewhere—in another part of downtown or another city, another country even—charged everything I saw and did with a secret glamour, the expectation that at any minute he might walk into CBGB or Club 82, or crawl from the wreckage of a party in some decaying loft. Photographing Quinn altered the way I saw the world. He was the lens that made everything darker, even as it brought it all into painfully sharp focus. It wasn't love but something stronger: a sense of immanence, of being on the edge of some revelation that drove me to arm myself with a cheap camera and black-and-white film. That feeling stayed with me throughout my early years in the city. It charged my best work. Even if no one else could see Quinn's gaze reflected in a broken syringe or a bathroom mirror at last call, I could.

But gradually that sense faded, or I did. I felt flickers of it sometimes, if I was drunk enough. Like now.

I retrieved his photo from my bag and stared at that bruised gaze, at once defiant and slightly desperate. I had always thought I'd known how that story ended. Prison, then . . .

What? The boy in that photograph was as dead as the girl who'd been behind the camera. But somewhere, the man Quinn O'Boyle had become had found that picture. He'd found me.

I put away the photo. The music stopped; my boots echoed loudly as I headed to the bar. Ritva looked up from a magazine.

"Another?"

"No thanks." I held up the card William Lindblad had given me that morning. "There a phone I could use?"

She slid a phone across the counter, and I made my call.

"Helsingin Taksi."

I gave him the bar's address. The cab arrived a few minutes later, still blaring Wagner, and Lindblad nodded as I climbed in.

"Back to Ullanlinna?"

"Airport."

"You should like this," he yelled, backing out of the alley. "Valkyries. Like you." He jabbed at my reflection in the rearview mirror, then touched the outer corner of his eye. "That scar, right? You're going home already? Helsinki in the winter is not a lot of fun. That's why you should try Disneyland."

"Next time I'll remember that," I said, and braced myself as we careened out of town.

10

There were only two flights a day to Reykjavík. Icelandair wouldn't let me pay cash, so I was stuck with a smaller operation that appeared to service vacation destinations near the Arctic Circle. No one seemed to want my money. When I tried to trade some of my euros for krónur at the currency exchange, the woman gave me a bored look.

"We don't do krónur."

"Is there anyplace else?"

"No one is doing krónur."

I found a quiet corner, finished my Jack Daniel's, then went through security. I got checked out thoroughly, presumably because I'd just paid cash for a one-way ticket to a country so broke it made me look like Bill Gates, if Gates traveled coach on a plane that had rolled off the assembly line back when Bono meant Sonny. The flight was nearly empty—four Japanese girls, a few people I assumed were Icelandic because they smiled more than the Finns, and me.

I dozed fitfully for several hours, woke when we hit some turbulence and one of the Japanese girls behind me started hyperventilating. I looked out the window and saw a shimmering archipelago of lights far below—Iceland's coast. A few minutes and the lights were gone. I searched for some other sign of life below us, but there was nothing. I fell back asleep and dreamed of gazing at an immense photographic negative, a vast sheet of black glass that splintered at my touch.

It was past midnight when we finally touched down. The Keflavik airport was empty, except for a single clerk at Border Control. I exited into what seemed like an abandoned shopping mall—shuttered duty-free shops, deserted seating areas, empty escalators moving up and down. The currency exchange was closed, and when I tried to use an ATM, it refused to convert my euros into krónur. I wondered what the black-market rate was for foreign money.

Outside, a solitary bus idled in the pouring rain. The driver asked for a ticket. I gave him a couple of bills and clambered on board.

The trip to Reykjavík was like a bus tour through Mordor. Black lava fields, an endless waste broken here and there by ruined machinery or a building of stained corrugated metal. No trees. No towns. No stars, no moon; nothing but black sky above and desolation below. Occasionally a streetlight shone through the rain, ominous as a UFO. Desultory '70s music dribbled from the radio between the rhythmic shriek of the wiper blades. The Japanese girls tried in vain to get a cell-phone signal. One of them staggered on tippy-toe heels to the front of the bus and asked the driver about the northern lights.

"Not cold enough," he said.

Finally we reached a stretch of suburban strip malls—gas stations, fast-food joints, an Icelandic megastore—and pulled onto a spur road into the city. At the bus station I followed the Japanese girls into a minivan that took us downtown. Narrow streets crowded with SUVs and Audis; sidewalks even more crowded with drunken kids. The van stopped in the middle of what looked like the main drag, where a neon HOTEL sign glowed above a metal awning. The girls straggled out, retrieved their luggage, and went inside. The driver looked at me.

"Where to?"

I realized I had no idea where to stay. I was too exhausted to think of looking for Quinn, too tired even to find a bar. I pointed at the hotel awning. "This place expensive?"

"Yes." The driver leaned out the window to spit.

I stared through the rain at a guy who repeatedly pushed his weeping girlfriend against a wall. Behind us, a car horn blared.

"How about someplace quiet?" I asked. "And cheap."

"Cheap?" The driver eased the van forward. "In Reykjavík?"

"Just as long as I'm not sleeping in the bus station."

We crept past more drunks, another guy shoving around his girlfriend, a huddle of teenagers smashing beer bottles against the curb. "Is it always like this?"

"Everything is worse now." The driver swore as a boy lurched across the street, oblivious of oncoming traffic. "You chose a bad time to visit."

The van turned down one side street, then another, and at last drew up in front of a nondescript corner building. White stucco had flaked away in patches, revealing gray cement mottled as lichen. Limp curtains hung inside grit-spattered windows.

"Hotel Kátur," the driver announced.

Inside, a worn modular sofa was pushed against one wall, its cushions faded to the same dingy gray as the cement exterior. There were stacks of tourist brochures on a battered coffee table, an empty beer bottle, and one wool glove. Everything reeked of disinfectant and cigarette smoke.

"*Halló, gott kvöld.*"

I turned to see a middle-aged man behind a small counter.

"Yeah, I'm looking for a room."

"Okay." He set a clipboard on the counter and pointed at a rate sheet in English. "Just one night?"

"For now, anyway." I pulled a few bills from my wallet. "Euros okay?"

He nodded, handed me a key, and pointed to a stairwell. Upstairs, I found my room, tossed my jacket and boots on the floor, and fell into bed.

I awoke to the sound of a truck idling outside. I checked the time on the bedside clock. A bit after ten, but was that morning or night?

I stood, head pounding, staggered to the bathroom, and forced myself to drink several glasses of sulfurous water, which made me throw up. I felt slightly better after I took a scalding shower that stank of rotten eggs. Then I dressed and went downstairs. The same man was behind the counter, hunched in front of a laptop.

"It's supposed to snow, maybe," he said without looking up.

"There a place where I can get coffee and something to eat?"

He pointed at the door, flicked his hand to the right. "That way. Laugavegur." I traded him some euros for krónur and stepped outside.

The street acted like a wind tunnel for the gale blowing from the harbor. I'd forgotten my watch cap, so did my best to cover my ears and face with my scarf as I hurried uphill. I'd gone only a few steps when a piercing cry rang out behind me. I looked back.

Whirling white shapes filled the black sky above the harbor: a cyclone of seagulls and wild geese, thousands of them rising and falling as though trapped inside a huge snow globe. I watched, mesmerized, until the cold got too much for me, then turned and trudged up the street.

There seemed to be more birds than people in this place. I didn't see another person. No dogs or cats, either, and not a lot in the way of vegetation, besides some shrubs and depressed-looking birch trees. Apart from the cries of seabirds, the city felt muffled. I started at the sound of horses' hooves, then saw it was an SUV, its studded tires ringing against the cobblestones.

And the air had no smell. No exhaust. No smoke. No dog shit or rancid grease from fast-food joints, none of the city reek and fume you absorb without knowing.

But also no green smells, trees or grass or wet earth. I couldn't even smell the ocean, close as it was. The city was a kind of sensory tabula rasa.

I reached Laugavegur, a deserted street lined with shops that offered some protection from the wind. Spindly evergreens were strung with forlorn fairy lights. The blocky buildings looked like cheap toys, their colors slightly off—sallow green, brownish red, baby-shit yellow. I passed a shuttered tattoo parlor, a vacant art gallery, a bar.

Dust-covered vitrines filled an abandoned jewelry store. The evergreens turned out to be lampposts, the fairy lights arranged to mimic the shape of Christmas trees. In a darkened boutique, bald mannequins wore artfully distressed clothing. I squinted to read the sale price on a tattered T-shirt. ÚTSALA 400,000 KR. What a fucking deal. Nobody was buying. Block after block, SALE and FOR RENT signs flapped in the wind. ÚTSALA! TIL LEIGA. A string of Christmas lights formed a noose around a plastic Viking doll. Shattered glass glittered on the sidewalk, broken beer bottles, broken headlights. It was like a scene from a disaster movie, a city everyone had fled after the plague struck.

After a few minutes I reached a stretch that seemed relatively prosperous, with clubs plastered with gig posters, several jewelers, and a few shops catering to tourists, their windows filled with Lopi sweaters, toy puffins, reindeer-hide mittens. A pizza joint, only open for dinner. Across the street, a metal sidewalk sign rattled in front of a dingy corner diner. A sudden gust sent the sign flying. I dodged it and hurried inside.

The room smelled reassuringly of coffee and fried fish. A few people huddled at the counter; others sat at scuffed tables beside the windows. I found an empty table in the back, a chair repaired with electrical tape. A platinum-haired girl wearing a sweater knit from what looked like green yak fur came over and handed me a menu.

"You got one in English?" I asked.

"Yeah, sure." She flipped it over. I ordered fried eggs and sausages and coffee, for about what my flight over here had cost. A shot of bourbon would have covered the return ticket, so I decided to hold off for the nonce.

79

The breakfast reminded me of that line from *Quadrophenia* about fried eggs making you sick first thing in the morning. Still, the coffee was good.

"Nice sweater," I said when the waitress returned to clear the table.

She stuck the bill under my coffee mug. "My boyfriend gave it to me."

I wondered if her boyfriend had bought it from Bigfoot. I dropped some cash on top of the check. "I'm supposed to meet a friend here, but he hasn't shown up. An American."

"What's he look like?"

I frowned. What *did* he look like? "About my age," I said at last. "Guy named Quinn O'Boyle."

The girl surveyed the room. "I don't think so. Only a few people have been in here."

"You sure?"

"Yeah." She tilted her chin toward the counter. "Want me to ask?"

"That'd be great. Quinn O'Boyle."

She went behind the counter and stuck her head into a pass-through piled with dirty plates, yelled at someone, then turned to wave me over. "Ask Andrés; he's here more than I am."

A burly man strode from the kitchen. Grizzled reddish hair topped by a black ski cap, beard flecked with cigarette ash, face weathered to the color of raw meat by sun and wind. His stained apron featured a picture of Jamie Oliver embellished with horns and a Hitler mustache.

"Yeah?" He smelled strongly of fish.

"I'm looking for a guy named Quinn O'Boyle. I was supposed to meet him a little while ago, and . . ." I shrugged.

"O'Boyle?"

I nodded. Andrés stared at me, his expression impossible to read. After a moment he looked over his shoulder and shouted into the kitchen, then cocked a thumb toward a dim staircase. "Come on."

Upstairs was a bigger dining room with grimy windows overlooking the street. Andrés kicked open a door behind a karaoke deck and stepped out onto a fire escape. He propped the door with a chair and dug into his apron pocket for a pack of cigarettes. "Can't even fucking smoke inside a fucking bar anymore."

He held the pack out to me. I shook my head and he lit up, leaned against a precarious railing, and stared down into a driveway crammed with trash bins and empty liquor cartons.

"Fucking nanny state. You American? Americans all think they're going to live forever. You're fucking going to die of something." He exhaled and turned his back to the wind. "I know Quinn the Eskimo. The Mighty Quinn."

"Is he American?"

"Canadian, I think. Maybe American." His breath mingled with the smoke. "Are you his sister?"

"Not if he's Canadian. Or an Eskimo." I tried to find a place out of the wind, gave up, and leaned against the door.

"You look like him." Andrés tossed his cigarette and reached into his apron pocket. He withdrew his hand and opened it to display a mass of something white and glistening. I caught a whiff of putrefying fish as he tossed the lump into the air. A brilliant white gull dove to snatch the fish and soared off before I could draw a breath.

"Arctic tern—it should have migrated months ago. Hungry little bastard," said Andrés. "They'll attack if you go near their nests." He stared admiringly into the empty sky.

"In Helsinki I saw a talking raven."

"I have never seen that." Andrés lit another cigarette. "But the Finns—they're sorcerers. In the old days, that's what they said. The Finns are sorcerers, like we are Vikings. The men, anyway." He pinched the match out between his fingers. "Old women are witches. And some young ones I know, too." He laughed.

"Like Valkyries?"

"Sure. Valkyries talk to ravens, too. In the sagas. 'We sisters weave our cloth with the entrails of men, their severed heads: corpse carriers, our bounty chosen from the bodies of the slain.'"

He turned, and a spill of light struck one side of his face. Shadows sheared away the rest, save for a scatter of what looked like glitter across his cheek. His cell phone rang, and he stepped away to answer it. When he returned, I saw that the glitter on his face was fish scales.

"Back to work. I haven't seen Quinn in a while. He moves around, but usually he comes into the bar. He used to be at Sirkus every night, before the motherfuckers tore it down."

"Is there someplace else he hangs out?"

"Yeah. Every bar in Reykjavík." He stepped toward the door. "Viva Las Vegas—he's there a lot."

I followed him downstairs. Andrés headed for the kitchen and stopped. "What's your name? In case I see him?"

"Just say an old friend."

"How good a friend?" I didn't reply. Andrés stared at me, then lowered his voice. "You should be careful. It's a small place, Reykjavík. Easy to find someone here. But outside the city, it's easy to get lost for a long time."

I nodded, pulled up the collar of my leather jacket, and stepped back into the cold.

11

Viva Las Vegas was an overheated casino bar where the morning gamblers clutched slot machines so avidly it looked like they were having sex with them, an impression bolstered by the groans that erupted every time someone won or lost big. I angled between people waiting for a turn at the slots. Judging from their grim faces and sunken eyes, most of them had been there for a while—years, maybe. I wondered how many people died at the machines and whether they just tossed the bodies into a cold back room and waited till spring to bury them.

I scanned the room for someone who resembled Quinn. I tried running a fast-forward, time-lapse loop in my head. The pale-skinned boy who used to sprawl across his mattress and stare at me with hostile eyes: I could no more imagine that boy than I could imagine my seventeen-year-old self inside the gaunt, scarred creature I'd become.

I gave up and grabbed a seat at the bar. A plasma TV played a music video with the sound turned off, a singer in a dolphin mask backed by blue-faced people in space suits. The bartender sang along in Icelandic.

I ordered a beer and got something called Gull. The whole fuck-

ing country was like *The Birds*, if the birds had won. I drank and
thought about what Andrés had said: a guy named Quinn, Canadian
or maybe American; a guy who looked like me.

It had to be him. Quinn and I used to lie in bed with our hands
pressed together, then our arms; chest to breast, groin to groin,
aligning ourselves as though we stared into a mirror. His hair red,
mine tawny, his eyes fern green and mine gray ice. I flagged down
the bartender.

"Another beer?"

"In a minute. A friend's supposed to meet me, a guy named
Quinn. Is he around?"

"Not all week." The bartender was short, with hennaed hair
and a sunburst tattooed on her wrist. "Dagny's over there, you
could ask her."

She tipped her head toward a very tall woman bent over a slot
machine, white-blond braids framing her angular face. She wore a
tight red T-shirt and expensive jeans tucked into fur-trimmed boots.
Icelandic Casino Barbie. I left some money on the bar and walked
over.

"Dagny."

The woman stared at the icons flickering across the screen as
though they measured her vital signs. She cursed and fed more
money into the machine without glancing at me.

"I'm looking for Quinn. Is he around?"

"*Farðu i rassgat.* Go fuck yourself."

I kicked the slot machine. It flickered then flashed try again. The
blond woman whirled, fist raised to strike. I grabbed her wrist and
wrenched her toward me. "I'm looking for Quinn. Is he around?
Simple question."

She pulled away, nearly yanking my arm from its socket, and I let go. She straightened and looked at me dead-on, her face a rictus of fury.

I returned her glare but took a step back. I wasn't used to meeting women eye to eye. She was older than I first thought but still younger than me, her face seamed with lines, none of them produced by smiling.

"Who the fuck are you?" she spat.

"An old friend."

She stared at me, then laughed harshly. "Then I can ask you the same thing: Where's Quinn? Stupid fucking question." She stooped to pick up a lipstick-red handbag. "I don't know. He owes me fifty thousand krónur. He sold some stuff for me and now he's holding out...."

Instinctively I looked at her arm. Telltale reddened pockmarks, like fleabites, and an abscess near the crook of her elbow. She caught my glance and bared her teeth in disdain.

"Fuck you. I gave him a bunch of old vinyl; he sells it on eBay. If you find him, tell him he still owes me fifty thousand krónur."

"Where could I find him?"

She pushed a blond strand from her face. "Kolaportið maybe. I checked the last two weeks, but he wasn't there. And I'm leaving for Uppsala this afternoon, so..." She shook her head. "I'll find him when I get back. Asshole."

"Where's Kolaportið?"

She leaned forward and gave me a shove that sent me reeling, turned, and stalked off. When I caught my balance, she was gone.

I made my way back to the bar and ordered another Gull. The silent flat-screen had switched from Cetacean MTV to BBC

World. The bartender poured herself a mug of coffee, yawning.

"What's Kolaportið?" I asked her.

"Kolaportið? That's the indoor flea market down by the harbor. It used to be the coal warehouse. Big building."

"Is it far from here?"

"Nothing is far in Reykjavík. Just walk toward the harbor, that way." She gestured vaguely at the wall. "But it's not open today. Only weekends. Tomorrow."

"Tomorrow's Saturday?"

I drank my beer. I felt trapped in some bizarre time loop where the clock had stopped and the sky never turned to dawn. The background noise was nothing but electronic *chings*, the nonsense susurrus of a language I didn't understand, or want to. Even the oldest burnouts here were younger than me. I was wasting my time along with the remaining stash of money Anton had sent me. I had a valid passport and some ready cash: I could have gotten a flight to Greece or Ibiza. Instead I was holed up near the Arctic Circle in the Casino of the Living Dead.

I glanced at the soundless TV. A woman newscaster stood in a rainy street, talking to another woman with a drawn face. Behind them a crowd of newspeople and cops mingled among emergency vehicles and flashing lights. A man strode past in a blue polisi windbreaker, followed by another cop with a German shepherd on a leash. A caption crawled across the screen: fashion murder.

I leaned forward. The TV crowd began to scatter, warned off by a cop with a soundless bullhorn. As people dispersed, I could see where police tape sealed off the perimeter of a tidy front garden. A grim-faced man hurried up the steps behind a tall woman in a gray suit, who, in a movie, would be the chief police investigator.

Only this wasn't a movie. It was Ilkka's house.

"What the hell." I waved at the bartender. "Hey—can you turn that up?"

She hit the volume and walked away. At the other end of the bar stood a youngish, well-heeled blond guy in a D&G pin-striped suit, a dark green overcoat slung across his shoulder. He downed a shot and stared at the screen.

". . . after last night's murder of a former *Vogue* photographer in an upscale Helsinki neighborhood. Police say Ilkka Kaltunnen and his assistant were found dead in his office by his wife when she returned home from an appointment. There are no details as to the murders, no indications yet if burglary was the motivation behind the early-evening slayings, although Kaltunnen's office and a downstairs work area were ransacked."

The newscaster signed off, and the screen filled with recent unemployment figures. The bartender picked up my empty glass. "You want another?"

I shook my head and tossed some krónur on the counter. The blond guy turned and looked at me, then back at the TV. I headed for the door fast as I could without breaking into a run, convinced that every hollow-eyed gambler would stare after me and scream for the police.

No one lifted an eyelash. I left the bar as anonymously as I'd entered it, stumbling back into the dark street. I wrapped my scarf around my face and zipped up my jacket as far as it would go.

I knew this was crazy paranoia. No one would recognize me. No one in this city knew who I was; no one cared about a dead photographer fifteen hundred miles away. I had a feeling it wouldn't just be crazy paranoia for long.

12

I hurried toward the harbor, sleet buffeting me in horizontal waves. I guessed it was mid-morning: The gray sky looked as though someone had turned the dimmer switch up a notch. Above the sea loomed a massive wall of cloud, banded asphalt gray and basalt. I thought of Ilkka, of blood in a blank white corridor, and felt dizzy. Horror, but also desolation at the loss of his gift, that terrible eye for the beauty in extinction.

Something shrieked: I looked up to see the same kind of bird I'd seen earlier with Andrés, luminous white against the lowering clouds. It fought against the gale, eerily suspended in place, until the wind shifted and it shot above the rooftops. When it disappeared, I grimly replayed the TV news in my head.

There'd been no mention of how Ilkka and Suri had been killed, or precisely when. I tried to remember what Ilkka had told me before he left—that his wife was in a meeting, that he'd pick up his son at school, take him to the doctor if he was sick. We would have dinner together later.

Despite the cold, sweat beaded on the back of my neck. Was it supposed to be me dead, and not Suri? Ilkka's office had been ransacked, and a workroom. I'd bet my Konica that among the missing were the Jólasveinar photos.

Yet Ilkka had insisted that not even his wife knew about those pictures.

I stopped at the verge of the busy road beside the harbor. The sky had taken on an ominous, mineral-green tinge. I waited for a break in the traffic and ran through a slurry of snow and grit, kept running until I reached the water's edge. I picked my way among rocks and tidal pools, fighting panic. Suri claimed she'd never been downstairs. No one had ever stepped foot into Ilkka's sanctum but me. No one but me knew those photos were there. . . .

Anton.

What had I told him?

"He's got a whole Batcave downstairs. Nice darkroom."

". . . someone else who was interested. A guy, from Oslo, maybe? Someone with very deep pockets."

"Ilkka and I have a deal," Anton had said. *"You might remind him of that."*

Anton hadn't made Ilkka a better offer. He'd simply offed him, ransacked the place, grabbed the Yuleboy prints, and fled. That, or he'd planned all along to take out me and Ilkka, hiring someone else who'd mistaken Suri for Cassandra Neary.

By now, they'd know they'd fucked up, and that I was still alive. I stared at the mass of clouds that filled the sky above the North Atlantic.

They weren't clouds. Above the horizon towered a mountain of jagged flint-gray rock, seamed with crevasses white-streaked with snow. No vegetation, buildings, or power lines, nothing but that menacing promontory and the waste of ice and darkness beyond—the beginning of the end of the world.

13

I have no memory of returning to my hotel, just the heat that enveloped me when I finally got inside. A different guy was behind the counter, a young black kid who stared intently at an iPhone. He glanced up, and I handed him enough krónur to cover another night.

"Is there a computer I could use to check my e-mail?"

He nodded and ducked down to retrieve a laptop. "Just give it back when you're done."

I settled on the sofa, booted up, and searched for coverage of Ilkka's murder.

I found a bunch of news items in Finnish and Swedish, photos of Ilkka, and one of Suri. A brief AP piece; another in *Paris Match* with thumbnails of Ilkka's fashion photography. Nothing in *The New York Times* or other U.S. press. Too early, maybe, or too much bad news to compete with. I finally hit the jackpot with an article in that morning's *Guardian*.

DOUBLE MURDER SHAKES FASHION WORLD

HELSINKI: Noted Finnish photographer Ilkka Kaltunnen and his assistant were found dead yesterday in his residence in an affluent Helsinki neighborhood, victims of a brutal murder. The bodies of Kaltunnen, 39, and Suri Kulmala, 30 and a former model, were discovered by Kaltunnen's wife when she returned home from work. Kaltunnen was found in the hall outside his office, his skull crushed by a silver serving dish. A few feet away, Kulmala's body lay sprawled in the office entrance, her neck broken when the door closed upon it hard enough to sever her spinal column. Kaltunnen's wife was with their young son at the doctor's office at the time of the killings. Her husband had returned home to attend to a business matter.

Speculation as to a possible romantic relationship between the two was dismissed as "utter nonsense" by someone close to Kaltunnen and his wife, a child psychologist. Police say that robbery was the more likely motive, but would not confirm whether any valuables were missing. Kaltunnen had amassed a substantial collection of twentieth-century photographs, including masterworks by Robert Mapplethorpe and Arthur Fellig, better known as Weegee. A basement darkroom had also been ransacked.

Neighbors professed shock that such a thing could happen in one of Europe's safest cities, while the fashion world mourned the loss of an icon, albeit one who had kept a low profile for the last decade. "He was a genuine visionary," proclaimed Grace Coddington, creative director of U.S. *Vogue*, "one of the earliest artists to embrace digital photography and . . ."

I skipped the rest and sat staring at the screen. Finally I cleared the laptop's history and returned it to the hotel clerk.

"Nobody left a message for me, right?" I asked. "No one came by or anything?"

He shook his head. "No. It's been quiet all morning."

The upstairs corridor was empty, with the same dank odor of mildew and cleaning fluid. I stepped into my room and turned the dead bolt, pulled down the window shades, and collapsed onto the bed.

It had to have been Anton—him or someone he'd paid off. A wealthy collector and dealer of murderabilia would presumably have contact with the kind of people who made his hobby possible. It would take someone a lot stronger than me to bash in Ilkka's skull and snap Suri's neck in a slammed door.

Had Anton planned the murders from day one? Or was he just so enraged by the thought of Ilkka selling the photos to someone else that he jumped in before the transaction could take place? Whichever it was, he'd now be aware that Suri Kumala had been killed and not Cassandra Neary. Maybe he'd look for me in New York.

Or maybe he wouldn't look for me at all. Maybe I was just spinning out the kind of paranoid fantasy you come up with after tweaking or bingeing for a week.

Only thing was, I'd been relatively sober, for me.

I pulled off my soaked cowboy boots and threw them in a corner along with my jacket. I wished I'd thought of finding a liquor store; I was afraid to leave my room, until I came up with something like a plan. That was going to be tough. I don't believe in safety nets: I believe in trapdoors, and the kind of luck that looks like forward planning only if you're wasted enough to see a pattern in blood and broken glass.

Unfortunately, I wasn't that wasted yet. I rubbed my eyes and gazed at the dark window. Would INTERPOL be involved already? Ilkka might have told his wife he'd had a visitor, but she wouldn't have known why I was there. Suri knew who I was, but she was dead. The bartender had seen me, and so had the cab driver. Neither of them knew my name, though they might remember a tall American woman in a hurry to leave Helsinki.

Still, I wasn't in a rush to go back to New York. People were already on my ass about Aphrodite Kamestos's death, plus Anton might have arranged for his friends to meet me. In Iceland a six-foot blond probably wouldn't draw much attention. If I kept my mouth shut, I might be able to pass as a native.

I couldn't stay at this hotel: Both clerks would have clocked me as an American. But I had nowhere else to go. The only thing I knew was that I had to find Quinn and lie low. I downed a Vicodin and hoped that Anton Bredahl didn't have a lot of friends in Reykjavík.

When I woke I felt better, until I remembered where I was. I'd slept almost sixteen hours. The snow had stopped. I showered and dressed, popped two Focalin, grabbed my bag, and went downstairs. The middle-aged clerk stood outside on the sidewalk, his cigarette glowing in the morning dark. There was no way to leave without walking past him, so I pulled on my watch cap and went out. He averted his eyes as I left.

I walked up to Laugavegur. The wind had died; the raw air felt almost balmy. Church bells chimed as a cop on a motorcycle buzzed past. I went to the place I'd had breakfast the day before, but it was closed, chairs stacked atop the tables inside, a fetid smell of beer and spoiled fish around the entrance. From an apartment across the street echoed a thumping bass line, joined intermittently by drums that couldn't keep the beat. Band practice.

I kept going. At the end of the next block I stopped to stare at some official-looking buildings. A few lights shone in the windows of Legoland houses and apartment complexes, their architectural details lost in the murk. Everything looked grainy and underexposed. If Reykjavík had been a photographic print, I would have tossed it.

I headed for the harbor, where droning boat engines drowned out the hum of traffic, and an iodine glare stained the sky above blocks of unfinished construction. Skeletal high-rises; piles of black gravel and rusted beams; pits surrounded by scaffolding and sonotubes. Graffiti covered plywood barricades. A tarp hung from a girder like a spiral of blackened skin. It resembled some futurist ruin, all that remained of a city sacrificed to the god that had abandoned it.

I got out my camera and picked my way among chunks of concrete and plywood walkways. The wind stung my face, but I hardly noticed: I was rapt, sucked into that place where the vision inside my head merged with what was in front of me. I shot half a dozen frames, and for a few minutes I forgot about everything except for the world inside my viewfinder.

In the last hour the city had awakened. Molten sunlight set steel girders and I beams ablaze as a decrepit orange bus jounced by in a cloud of exhaust, empty except for its driver. I put away my camera and set out to find the flea market.

Along the shore a couple walked hand in hand, a skein of gulls trailing them like smoke. Live music—more band rehearsals— wafted down streets corrugated with frozen slush. I found a crowded hot dog stand where I waited in line with bleary-eyed kids who passed around cigarettes as they kicked at the broken tarmac. I picked up an occasional word or phrase in their hangover chatter—band names, mostly. I bought two hot dogs and, when I was done eating, approached a boy wearing a pink-and-green anorak and matching Vans shoes.

"I'm looking for Kolaportið."

He gestured at a nondescript white building that took up most of a block. "Over there."

I crossed the street, walked through a parking lot filled with people unloading cars and pickups, and went inside. There was already a small mob, so I waited between a wizened man in a cowboy hat and a dumpy woman flanked by three kids squabbling over a Game Boy. Another man guarded a rope that separated us from a cavernous, table-filled space flooded with acrid fluorescent light. People jostled past me, and Cowboy Hat shook his head reproachfully until the rope dropped and the crowd dispersed.

Inside was the usual flea-market crap: fast-food toys marketed as collectibles, pirated slasher movies from Indonesia, homemade jewelry, tapestries emblazoned with dolphins or Michael Jackson, used appliances, old paperbacks. It was like the gods of commerce had swallowed all this stuff, then puked it up again. The only thing that marked this as a flea market in Reykjavík rather than Rockville was the glut of woolen clothing. You name it, somebody's Icelandic grandmother was perched on a folding chair, knitting it while she kept a cool eye on the competition across the aisle.

At least it was crowded, which would make it harder for someone to find me. Harder, too, for me to find Quinn. How the hell would I recognize him? Half the middle-aged men here looked like they'd had the life Quinn probably ended up with: gazes blunted by drugs or alcohol; gray hair, bad teeth, thinning ponytails; stained relaxed-fit cargo pants, Bob Marley T-shirts pulled over slack bellies.

I made a circuit of the room and ended at an indoor café with plastic tables and a take-out window. The old man in a cowboy hat had set up an electronic keyboard and was singing Roy Orbison songs. Not bad, either. I checked out the delicatessen area, which was big on food that looked like doggie chew toys—dried fish and the heads of quadrupeds in varying stages of decay. I passed on the free samples and made another loop of the market.

Most of the faces were familiar from my first go-round. Anxiety crept into my frustration as I considered the notion that Quinn and Ilkka's killer were the same person, which would at least consolidate my growing paranoia. I paused at a bookstall whose proprietor ignored me to speak animatedly into his cell phone. To one side of the bookstall, a woman with close-cropped black hair presided over a makeshift grotto filled with carven animals, handmade leather pouches, and stones painted with runes. Beside her, two teenage girls hawked tie-dyed clothing to a man in an expensive-looking loden-green overcoat. He looked slightly out of place among all the schlubby jumble salers: expensively shaggy dark-blond hair, pinstriped trousers, nice leather shoes ruined by road salt. It was a second before I twigged that it was the same guy I'd seen standing at the bar in Viva Las Vegas.

He must have sensed me watching him: He turned and fixed me with the dispassionate gaze of a fox distracted from the hunt. I stared back. A mistake, but I'd never seen eyes that color before—not on a human being—so pale a brown they were almost topaz. He raised his hand as though to beckon me over.

"Hey," he said. Good English, but not a native speaker. "Are you lost?"

I darted off, ducked behind a display, and kept going till I reached a crowded aisle. I stopped beside a long table and scanned the room but didn't see him.

"*Góðan dag.*" Behind the table, a young guy unpacked a cardboard box. He was very thin, with blanched white skin, a mass of silvery curls, and ruby eyes that glowed like votive candles behind thick-lensed glasses. An albino. "*Hvernig gengur?*"

I looked to see what he was unpacking—eight-track tapes. Dagny had said that Quinn sold old vinyl. I picked up and then immediately dropped an eight-track of the Starland Vocal Band. The albino gave me a cursory smile, settled into a chair, and began tapping on an iPad.

Crates covered the table. I peered into one that held scores of vinyl LPs, some new, others old but still shrink-wrapped, all arranged alphabetically. I flipped through Rory Gallagher, Art Garfunkel, Marvin Gaye, Gentle Giant, pulled out Gong's *Camembert Electrique*, sans shrink-wrap but in pristine condition. The albino nodded in approval.

"That's the one Pip Pyle played on, before he split for Hatfield and the North. There's some more rare stuff over there. . . ."

He pointed to the far end of the table, where a hand-lettered sign reading ESKIMO VINYL leaned against a tower of eight-tracks. "One with Elton Dean and Marc Charig, Lyn Dobson does some amazing sitar. Check it out."

"I thought those guys never recorded with Gong."

"It's a live bootleg of a gig they did in Paris in 1971."

He flipped through a crate of LPs as though it were a Rolodex, plucked out an album—plain black sleeve, no lettering—and handed it to me, pointing to a turntable. "You can listen there if you want."

The turntable was a vintage Philips 312, the same model I had in my apartment back in the city. Not top of the line even back in 1976, but it got the job done. This one had been pimped out with Bose headphones, a Graham 1.5 tonearm with a tungsten arm, and a stylus so fine I barely heard it kiss the vinyl. The recording quality wasn't great—you could hear background conversation and the clink of glasses—but it wasn't as bad as some bootlegs I've heard.

Not my taste, though. I slid the record back into the sleeve and returned it the crate. The albino raised his eyebrows. "What'd you think?"

"It's okay." I debated whether to ask about Quinn, decided I'd hold off for the moment. "Not really my thing, that's all."

"What're you into?" He picked up a dome magnifier and examined a packing list. "We have a lot of old-style punk. Bootleg of Johnny Thunders's *L.A.M.F.*, live at Max's. Joy Division, *Le Terme.*"

"Thanks, I've got those."

I perused what appeared to be the world's most complete collection of Cramps picture discs, including one that featured Poison Ivy in a a red velvet armchair, wearing a plastic tiara and not much else. This seemed more like what Quinn might have been listening to, circa 1979.

And the velvet chair reminded me of something. I shut my eyes for a moment, thinking.

Darkthrone was one of the bands Suri had mentioned. I found the crate holding the Ds. Between Danzig and the Dead Milkmen were several Darkthrone LPs and picture discs available in a range of colors, as long as you liked black. I selected one at random.

"Okay if I play this?"

The albino had clipped what looked like a pair of tiny telescopes onto his glasses and was examining a twelve-inch as though it was printed in cuneiform. He nodded absently. "Yeah, sure."

Darkthrone's lead singer sounded like he'd taken vocal lessons from Hasil Adkins. Most of the lyrics were in Norwegian, but I suspected I'd have no trouble understanding them if I'd been a fifteen-year-old boy with anger-management issues. Whatever he was saying, he seemed to mean it. The guitar work sounded like an electric razor jacked on ice. I gave the band props for that before removing the album from the turntable.

"There's some good Mayhem there, too." The albino indicated another carton. "And we do special orders."

Mayhem was another band Suri had mentioned. I got a good suss on their worldview from the song titles—"Chainsaw Gotsfuck," "Carnage," "Necrolust."

"Here's the original 1987 *Deathcrush*." The albino handed me an LP wrapped in Mylar. "By the way, I'm Baldur."

"Like the Norse god?"

He grinned. "Yeah. A joke—in Norse, Baldur is called 'The White One.' There were only a thousand copies of that demo, all hand-numbered. See?" He pointed to the sleeve—number 666. "That was Necrobutcher's own copy. That's what I was told, anyway."

I wondered if Necrobutcher's mother had christened him that, but a guy named Baldur probably wasn't the one to ask. "Can I listen to it?"

He shook his head. "Not that one. There's a 1993 reissue on CD; we don't have it, but it's easy to find. I don't even know why Quinn keeps that here. He'll never let it go. Ozzy Osbourne's manager offered us three thousand dollars, and Quinn said no."

"Quinn." I handed back the LP, trying to sound nonchalant. "So is he around?"

"Maybe today. Maybe tomorrow. He's been gone for a while. Excuse me," he said, and turned to a girl holding a copy of *Astral Weeks.*

I flipped through the rest of Mayhem's oeuvre. Their fashion sense was early Nazgul—black leather, white corpse makeup, stringy hair. KISS for depressives. Quinn had always been more of a classic Chuck Berry, Rolling Stones, New York Dolls kind of guy, but maybe prison had changed his musical taste, or maybe he aimed strictly for the collectors' market. After a minute I withdrew another LP: *Dawn of the Black Hearts.*

The cover was a color photograph of a young man in a blood-stained T-shirt and plaid flannel shirt, lying on the floor. A shotgun pointed at a hand slick with blood, and lying across the gun's stock was a blood-spattered carving knife. Blond hair swept back from a forehead that dissolved into a porridge of shattered bone and brain tissue. I squinted to read the logo on the bloody T-shirt.

I ❤ TRANSYLVANIA

Ilkka's photographs hadn't triggered my sense of damage, but this picture reeked of it. It was like walking into a room where there's a gas leak.

"It's a nasty picture, that one," said Baldur, returning from his customer. "Especially if you're not expecting it."

"Seems like it would have limited commercial appeal."

"Yes. It's revolting. That's another rare one Quinn doesn't want to sell. If we put it on eBay, we'd get some good money for it. Which right now, we could use."

"You don't worry about someone ripping them off?"

"Oh, sure. But Brynja . . ."

He pointed across the room, and I saw the woman in the New Age grotto watching us. "That's our guardian. My sister. "

"She's your sister?"

Baldur laughed. "Yeah, I know. We're not a family of albinos. Just me." He waved at the dark-haired woman, who fixed me with a thousand-yard stare before turning away.

"She doesn't look too happy to see me."

"She hates Quinn." Baldur picked up *Dawn of the Black Hearts.* "Probably she thinks you're one of his friends."

"Why does she hate Quinn?"

"You know." He shrugged. "So you've never heard *Black Hearts*?"

"Nope. But that's a real photo, right?"

"Oh sure. It's real." He tapped the cover. "That's Dead."

"I mean, it's not, like, Photoshopped or—"

"No—his name is Dead. Or was, until he killed himself. Then Dead was really dead. His Christian name was Per Ohlin. He was Mayhem's lead singer—not the first, but he did the vocals on *Black Hearts*. Their lead guitarist, Euronymous, owned a record store in Oslo, and that's where Dead pulled the trigger—after he used the hunting knife. Euronymous found the body. He ran out and bought a camera, then rearranged the body to make it look prettier, and took a photograph—that photograph. A few years later it showed up as the cover of this bootleg."

"Christ. Nice bunch of guys."

"Yes, very nice." Behind their thick lenses, Baldur's ruby eyes glittered. "Dead used to carry around a dead raven in a plastic bag. He liked the way it smelled. He'd bury his own clothes in the dirt, then wear them when he sang onstage. He was in love with being dead: That was his romance."

"Looks like it was consummated."

"He was not the only one. Euronymous was murdered by someone in his band. Then there were all the church fires, and some other stuff, too, stuff you never heard about. Very bad shit."

I stared at the grisly photo, thinking of Ilkka's sequence and what Suri had told me about the Oslo music scene. Not that Europeans have a lock on that kind of stuff. In rock and roll, the fine line between showbiz and psychosis can be summed up in two words: Phil Spector.

I said, "I guess that would be some very bad shit. This stuff big in Iceland?"

"There are fans, but no one takes it seriously. And there are no murders here in Iceland, even by black metal singers." He laughed. "Iceland is very safe, very tolerant. They are very anti-Christian, those Norwegian bands. That's why they like the old gods, Odin and Thor and Loki. And me! Baldur the Beautiful—that works good to pick up girls, you know?

"Here we have almost as many heathens as Christians, but nobody gets too worked up about it, you know? And the Satanists are ridiculous. Even the black metal bands know that. Now they are mostly heathens. Some Viking metal is very good, but the rest—songs about human sacrifice, Gorgoroth impaling sheep's heads onstage—it's too much. My sister says we should get rid of their albums, not just Mayhem—all those bands. And sometimes I think she's right, but it's worth too much money."

"What does Quinn think?"

"Quinn? Nothing like that bothers him. That's why they call him Quinn the Eskimo. He's a cold one."

He slipped back behind the table. I hung around for a few more minutes, hoping Quinn might materialize, but finally gave up and left. As I passed her stall, Brynja turned to stare after me, her eyes narrowed and lips mouthing words I was glad I couldn't hear or understand.

Before leaving the market I invested in a secondhand Icelandic sweater that was way too big but about a hundred bucks cheaper than anything else, then went to find a bar. Outside, the wind nearly knocked me over. I headed away from the center of town, trudging up one gray street after another, trying in vain to escape the gale. The sun showed fitfully, revealing shreds of sky that glowed a brilliant, lacquered blue before they were extinguished by scudding pewter clouds. I stared into passing cars and shop windows, slowed down at street corners, always hoping to recognize Quinn.

But everyone I saw looked nineteen: walking arm in arm, singing snatches of songs in Icelandic or English; huddled in doorways, smoking. I felt like a ghost in the Land of Youth. The few places that looked like they'd serve alcohol were shuttered or, in many cases, closed for good.

After about an hour I reached a desolate stretch of black gravel in the lee of more unfinished construction—high-rises surrounding a square pit filled with rust-colored water. The place was a dumping ground for bashed-in fuel tanks and discarded tires as big as wading pools. Three old men stood beside a fire in a metal bin, smoking cigarettes and watching me with reddened eyes. One shouted something in Icelandic. The others laughed. I kept going.

Up ahead, a heap of soiled mattresses had been pulled beside a row of abandoned box vans, minus their 18-wheelers. Flames leapt from a tower of huge radials, accompanied by plumes of greasy black smoke. I covered my mouth, coughing, and glanced back.

The three men were gone. A solitary figure strode quickly across the vacant lot, a tall man in a loden-green overcoat, blond head down against the wind, as incongruous here as he'd been in the market. He lifted his head to gaze at me, teeth bared in a smile, and reached for his pocket.

I turned and sprinted for the abandoned trailers, blinded by acrid smoke. A sudden gust sent me reeling. I caught my balance, saw a gap in the smoke, and staggered toward it. I'd gone only a few steps before someone grabbed me by the throat. I kicked out, but my assailant elbowed me so hard I doubled over, gasping. My knees gave way as he dragged me across broken asphalt, up a set of metal stairs, and into the black interior of a box van. My head struck the floor, and the darkness took me.

———

Much later I opened my eyes, blinking as I tried to focus on something, anything, in the dark. It was useless. There was a pervasive smell of mold beneath the stench of scorched rubber. I sat up, head aching, and inched across the floor until I bumped a wall. Someone touched my leg. Before I could scream a hand covered my mouth.

"Shhh. Listen . . ."

I froze. Whoever was beside me didn't move. After a long moment he exhaled and withdrew his hand. There was a soft click, and I shaded my eyes, dazzled by the glow of a lighter. I could just make out a silhouette in the darkness and braced myself against the wall as he reached toward me. A hand touched my cheek and gently tilted my face to the light.

"Cassie . . ."

Only two people have ever called me that. One was my mother, dead for almost half a century. My voice broke as I breathed the other's name.

"*Quinn.*"

14

The lighter's glow illumined hollow cheeks and spectral glints within black eye sockets. Only the whispered voice was unmistakably Quinn's.

"Stay quiet. I wanted to be sure it was you. Wait here."

The flame went out. I heard him stand, walk a few yards, and stop. With a grunt he tugged open the metal door, just enough to peer out. Then he pushed it up a few more inches and crawled from the trailer, waving me to follow. I scooted across the floor and clambered down. Quinn pulled me to him and slung his arm around my shoulder.

"Just stay with me," he said curtly, and guided me across the vacant lot.

The pile of tires smoldered beneath a night sky pricked with a few faint stars. A boy tossed rocks into the foul-smelling mass, turning to give us an incurious look.

"Head down," Quinn murmured.

To any casual onlooker we were a couple huddled together against the cold, hurrying by dreary low-rise apartment buildings and patches of snow-silted turf. Cars passed, pedestrians carrying grocery bags, a haggard woman pushing a stroller. After a while, Quinn dropped his arm. He stopped, lit a cigarette, and turned to me.

It was the first time I got a good look at him. A rangy man in a black leather jacket battered as my own, worn corduroy trousers, heavy work boots; thin but big-boned, with the economical motions of someone who's spent thirty years poised to turn on a dime and throw a punch. My initial impression of a skull wasn't far off. Gaunt face, eyes so deep-set I couldn't catch their color; head shaven to reveal a cross-shaped scar at the crown of his scalp, the result of an accident or maybe a primitive jailhouse scarification.

But there was no doubt about the deliberateness of the tattoo between his eyes—three vertical red lines—or those at the corners of his mouth, twin sets of black horizontal lines that formed a permanent, ghastly grimace.

"Inuit." He exhaled. "I lived in Barrow for a while."

"Quinn the Eskimo." I reached to touch his face. He stiffened, and I dropped my hand. "What do they mean?"

"They mean I killed a man."

We continued walking until we reached a parking lot. Quinn stepped past several late-model SUVs with ÚTSALA signs stuck beneath their wiper blades, halting beside an old Jeep Cherokee. The driver's door was dented, the rear fender tied on with a bungee cord. "Get in."

The car was filled with fast-food wrappers, empty Jolly Cola bottles, crushed cigarette packs. Quinn slid behind the wheel. Once out of town he drove fast, skidding on patches of ice and loose black scree. The long walk had burned off some of the shock of seeing him again, but every time I tried to frame a question, I was put off by that grim, scarred face.

"Are you going to tell me what's going on?" I said at last.

He lit a cigarette. "I got to the stall, and Baldur said an American woman had just been asking after me. Tall, kind of blond, black leather jacket and cowboy boots. I ran out looking for you, then saw you were being tailed."

"Who is he? What the fuck happened back there?"

"You tell me. Guy named Einar Broddursson, I thought maybe you picked his pocket or something."

"Who the hell is Einar Broddursson?"

"He's a dick. A high-level banker at Vandlega, which before the crash was the second-biggest bank in Iceland. His father managed a fish processing plant. Einar studied economics here at Bifröst University and got an advanced degree at Wharton. So instead of fishing, he learned to swim with the sharks and use pension plans for chum. He's one of the guys who put this place in the toilet, then kept flushing till the shit hit London."

"So why'd you jump me instead of him?"

"Einar's not a guy you want to mess with unless someone's got your back. A lot of his business contacts are in Moscow, and I can guarantee you that they did not go to Wharton. Plus I wasn't sure it was you."

"What gave it away?"

"Those cowboy boots. And your bag—that's the same bag you had in high school, right? You still got the same camera? Still seeing the world in black and white?"

"Pretty much."

"No digital for you, huh?" His mocking laugh hadn't changed, or his just-north-of-the-Bronx accent. "Same old Cass."

"This is all just so freaking bizarre." I touched his face, and this time he didn't flinch. "I was afraid you were dead."

"Nope. But not for lack of effort." One of the wiper blades was frozen. Quinn stuck his hand out the window to free it, and the Cherokee veered into the other lane. "Like that—"

He swerved to avoid a Flybus airport shuttle and laughed again. "I started keeping track once, of how many times I almost died. ODs, a couple times in jail. Getting caught outside in Barrow in January—that'll do you. After fourteen I lost count."

"What are you doing here?"

It was a while before he answered. I stared out at the volcanic landscape, serrated black tephra like row upon row of obsidian knives. Now and then a light shone from a house, distant as the stars.

Finally he said, "I was married a long time back, a girl I met in Anchorage. I guess it's twenty-three years now. She was crazy, and, you know, I'm not the best-adjusted guy on the block. She's Icelandic—from Höfn, in the east. Fucking beautiful place— glaciers and shit. Woods, which you don't really find here. And Emma was easy on the eyes, too. Anyway, we split up, but I'd become a legal resident by then, so I stayed. Can't go back to the old country: I burned all those bridges."

"How'd you find me?"

"I read about those murders and saw your name. I almost swallowed my gum. Maine, is that where you live now?"

"No. I'm still in the city. Downtown."

"Yeah? How's that working for you?"

"Not so good. It's changed. Rich people with little dogs, assholes from Wall Street. And Brooklyn. I hate it."

"Same thing happened here, only our assholes are from Borgartún. That's the quote-unquote 'financial district,' which is one— count it—one building where all the banks were. Some prime office space available there these days. Somebody should line all those bankers up and shoot them." He laughed bitterly. "Can you tell I'm American?"

We talked, and I could feel that same old black energy crackling between us as we parried over who knew more, who'd fucked more people, taken more drugs, lost more blood, forgotten more nights in a haze of hangovers and withdrawal. I watched Quinn's profile, lit red in the dashboard glow. You could run a blade through those tattooed lines and not draw blood. I thought of prison time, of whatever he'd done back in the States that had made it impossible for him to ever return. I wouldn't win this particular round. After a while I kept my mouth shut.

After half an hour, Quinn turned off the main highway. We drove down a gravel road to a bleak oasis in lavaland, several warehouse-like structures clustered around a cell tower, and pulled up beside a small building with corrugated metal siding painted an industrial blue.

"*Heim sætt heim*," Quinn announced. "Home sweet home."

Inside reminded me of those subway tunnels where the mole people live, hot and claustrophobic, the air thick with cigarette smoke and sulfur. There was a futon bed, dirty sheepskin rugs and clothes scattered across the floor, magazine photos and old album sleeves tacked on to bare drywall—Chuck Berry, Keith Richards, Aretha Franklin. A bong and empty beer bottles sat on a coffee table made of a piece of glass balanced on a huge tire rim.

"Help yourself." Quinn retrieved a beer from the fridge and walked into the bathroom. "There's some Brennivín on the table."

I passed on the Brennivín and opened plywood cabinets until I found a bottle of Pölstar vodka that smelled like butane. I poured some into a dirty glass and knocked it back, refilled the glass, then explored the rest of Quinn's place.

There wasn't much besides the living room and kitchenette and two closed doors, one for the bathroom. I opened the other door, revealing a long room jammed floor to ceiling with cardboard cartons filled with vinyl record albums—hundreds, maybe thousands of them. Also stacks of cardboard mailers, sheaves of Mylar and Bubble Wrap.

I stepped inside, shivering—there was no heat—and picked my way across the room to a metal desk crammed with sound equipment. A laptop and iPod dock, ranks of speakers wired into a gold-standard turntable, Bose headphones, a two-headed cassette deck, a vinyl-to-CD adapter. Beside the desk were more boxes crammed with 45s. A few were mint; most had sleeves the worse for wear, stained and scrawled with the names of previous owners.

But they were all the real thing, original pressings of *Anarchy in the U.K.*, Luke the Drifter's "On Trial," The Spades' "You're Gonna Miss Me."

"You know what that one is, right?" I looked over as Quinn crouched beside me. He took a 45 from my hand and delicately removed it from the sleeve. "Roky Erickson before the 13th Floor Elevators. The silver label, that's what you look for."

He tilted the 45 to the light, stood, and put it on the turntable. The tonearm might have had a surgical-quality diamond tip, but even that couldn't dispel the familiar hiss and pop as the needle hit the grooves. I leaned against a pile of boxes, shut my eyes, and listened.

For two minutes and thirty-three seconds we might have been back in Quinn's bedroom, bound to each other by the echo of a Gibson guitar. I felt his hand rest gently upon my head. It remained there until the song ended. Neither of us spoke; neither of us stirred, until Quinn finally removed the 45. I blinked as though I'd awakened from a deep sleep.

"So. You really do this," I said. "Sell all this stuff—all this vinyl."

"Yeah I sell it." His expression was guarded. "What'd you think?"

"I don't know. Your friend Einar—is this the kind of business you do with him?"

"Some." He turned to stare at the box of 45s. "C'mon," he said at last. "I'm freezing. I have to keep this room cold so the vinyl doesn't warp."

Back in the living room I parked myself in a chair, glancing at a square of black window. The glass shuddered with a sound like a series of muffled underground explosions.

"What's that?" I asked. "Night blasting?"

"The ocean. You can't see it, but it's only about a hundred yards away. That's why I like this place. Also, it's a lot cheaper than Reykjavík."

"So you can afford to keep the heat cranked."

"Everything's geothermal. Stick a pipe in the ground, you got heat. The AC is what costs." He got another beer and handed me the vodka bottle. "So what about you? What've you been up to for the last thirty years?"

"Not much." I refilled my glass. "Actually, I haven't done jack shit."

"No more photography?"

"I dunno. I tried, but nothing ever took off. I flamed out after my book, and then no one wanted to look me in the face."

"Try doing seven years in Otisville."

He lit a cigarette. Time had leached the color from his eyes: They were no longer spring green but a pale, cinereous gray. I waited for him to say something, to laugh or turn away or reach for me. Instead, he balanced the cigarette on the table edge and shucked off his flannel shirt and T-shirt.

My breath caught in my throat. Scars covered his chest, an intricate crosshatch of white and silvery gray that extended below his navel. A ragged gash ran along his right side; a knot of white scar tissue nestled in the hollow of his throat. As he breathed, his silvery flesh caught the light and seemed to shift, as though a net were being drawn across his skin. Tentatively I extended my hand, until my fingers grazed a scar on his left breast. A pattern of three interlocking shapes, like skeletal hands grasping each other, with a strange, masklike face at their center. At my touch, Quinn flinched and turned away.

"What happened to you, Quinn?" I whispered.

"Everything."

He sat, his gaze fixed on a dark lozenge of window; then he picked up his cigarette, leaned back in his chair, and closed his eyes. "God, I'm beat. I got up at four to drive down from Húsavik. I should have just let Baldur handle the stall."

"But then you wouldn't have found me."

"Good point." He opened his eyes and smiled slightly. "Welcome to Reykjavík."

I took a gulp of vodka. "That guy Einar—why was he chasing me?"

"You tell me, girlfriend. Mostly he just gets dressed like he's still going to work in Borgartún, then hangs around all day in a bar or some shit. Like me. Like everyone. The entire country's unemployed and on the verge of a psychotic breakdown." He pulled his flannel shirt back on. "You still haven't told me what the hell you're doing here."

"I don't know." I stared at the floor. "I guess I came to see you. That picture you sent me, with the news clipping. And the photo. I was just so blown away, to hear from you after all this time. I had no idea where you were."

"You had an idea, Cassie. You thought I was six feet under some boneyard." His gaze hardened. "Why didn't you ever write me? I got busted, and that was it: You threw me under a bus. Thirty years later, here you are like nothing happened."

"You took off with that chick in Harlem."

"Fuck that. You should've answered my letters, Cass."

I knew better than to argue or try to defend myself. I took another mouthful of vodka. "I thought you wanted me here. You don't, I'll split."

"Yeah? Where to? You gonna walk back to Reykjavík?" He shook his head. "Shit, it doesn't matter. Water under the fucking bridge. I did want you. I thought maybe you were dead, too." His skittery laugh echoed through the house. "Cute couple, huh? 'Most likely not to live past thirty.'"

"Well, we beat the odds."

"So you got my letter and just hopped a flight to Reykjavík?"

I toyed with my glass. "Not really."

I gave him an edited version of what had happened in the last few days—no details, just that I had some business in Helsinki and decided to make a side trip to Iceland.

"What kind of business?"

"Some photographs a guy wanted me to look at."

"Was it Anton?"

My hands went cold. "What?"

"The guy who hired you—was it Anton Bredahl? Norwegian guy."

"Uh, yeah," I stammered. "Yeah, it was Anton."

"That's good," said Quinn, almost to himself. "He mentioned a few weeks ago he was looking for a second opinion on some pictures. I read you were like this punk culture hero or something, you had that book. Turned out he knew who you were; he even had a copy. I told him I knew you when we were kids and he should get in touch with you. He throws around a lot of money, I figured you might as well get a taste. I went through all my old stuff to see if I had a letter, and all I found was that photo you took of me. Whatever happened to all those? But I thought, what the hell, I'd mail it to your old man's address in Kamensic. I didn't even know if he was still alive. I hoped maybe you might end up here," he added hesitantly. "If you got what I sent you."

"But—this is all just too fucking weird, Quinn." I stared into my glass. "How do you know Anton?"

"We move in the same circles. I'll tell you a little secret, girlfriend: You get out of the U.S., it really is a small world. For some things, anyway. Me and him go back a ways, before the Wall fell. Anton was in Leipzig; he was big into hardcore. Music." He laughed. "The other stuff, too. But music—everyone there wanted music, and they couldn't get it except on the black market. I was living here with Emma by then, so I'd go to Germany and arrange to get him stuff. No Internet—you had to do everything the old-fashioned way, smuggling in records and tapes and shit. But I knew this girl in West Berlin, her grandparents were in the East. Every time she visited them she'd hide some albums under the floor mat of her car."

"Jeez. Was she ever caught?"

"No, though once the heat from the engine melted them. I lost about a grand on that run. Whatever. After the Wall fell, Anton moved back to Oslo and opened a club. I was still establishing residency in Iceland and needed to keep it clean, so I started selling old vinyl by mail. When Kolaportið opened I got a stall there. Went online once the Internet came along. I had dupes of some seventies and eighties stuff; The Residents went for a lot. Thomas Dolby, not so much."

"Where's all your Chuck Berry?"

He smiled, and I glimpsed the seventeen-year-old Quinn behind the scrim of tattoos and scars. "Oh, I still have those: You don't fuck with Chuck. I get by. Anton's thrown me a bone or two over the years. And as you can see, I don't have a lot of overhead."

He stood to get another beer while I sat and tried not to be freaked by the fact that he knew Anton Bredahl. Though he hadn't shown a lot of curiosity about my own dealings with Anton—or about me, period—which fit with the Quinn I'd known, whose interests had never expanded much beyond junk and vinyl and sex. And maybe he was right; maybe the world got smaller and weirder when you lived abroad, the way downtown New York had gotten smaller and blander.

Still, in Reykjavík you'd have to move a lot of vinyl to make rent, and I suspected it wouldn't be enough to keep him in cigarettes and beer. Back in high school he'd sold dime bags of pot, along with Quaaludes and whatever he could get his hands on.

Those scars suggested he hadn't spent a lot of time in an office cubicle before relocating to Iceland.

"Hey." Quinn set his beer down, and reached to touch the scar beside my eye. "This looks new."

I said nothing. He leaned forward, drew my face to his, and kissed me. His lips were cracked, his hand on mine larger and rougher than it had been. But he smelled the same—smoke and sweat and beer—and his voice was the one I remembered from another world, another century.

"Cassie," he murmured.

It had been years since I'd been to bed with anyone, maybe a decade since I'd been with a guy; thirty-three years since that guy was Quinn O'Boyle. We were both drunk, so it took a while.

And we were both nearly silent, from shyness, or maybe fear that our voices might betray the younger selves locked inside the creatures we'd become. I traced the lines across his chest, the cross gouged into his scalp; Quinn but not Quinn, trapped within a sarcophagus of scar tissue. I recognized almost nothing except his eyes and the sound of my name whispered in the dark, his voice so soft I might have dreamed it.

But then I felt his hand on my breast. "Cassie. I can't believe you're here. Why did you leave me, Cassie?"

"I don't know," I whispered. "You were in jail. It was such a long time ago. People change. Everything changed."

"I didn't."

"No." I rolled over so that I could see him better. "You never did." My voice shook, and I looked away.

"It all might have been so different," said Quinn. "Instead of this. Now it's all too late."

"It was always too late," I said.

Afterward he fell asleep, and I watched the rise and fall of his ruined chest, the intertwined hands marking where his heart beat, his disfigured face even eerier in repose. Like one of those bodies dredged from a peat bog, its lost history tattooed upon weathered skin.

I leaned over to kiss his brow, rose, and crossed the room. I turned on a light and retrieved my camera, placed it on a chair to steady it, knelt, and gazed at him through the viewfinder.

He didn't stir. He was far more beautiful to me now than he had been all those years ago, asleep in some silent place where he'd escaped from whatever damage the world had written on him. I opened the camera's aperture and held the exposure for half a second, a lifetime, before pressing the shutter release. It sounded like a pistol shot, but Quinn didn't move.

I took several more pictures, then stopped, afraid of what might happen if he awoke and saw me once more behind a lens. More than that, I was afraid that this whole half-lit world would shiver into a dream of desire and loss, and I'd find myself back in my dark apartment, alone save for the blinking red eye of the answering machine. I stowed my camera and crept back into bed. When I finally slept, I dreamed of Quinn lying beneath dark water, seventeen again, his hair streaming around his face, and a blaze of pure white light erupting from the scars on his breast.

PART TWO

15

I awoke to a world still twilit, the sound of waves and rattle of sleet on metal. Beside me Quinn yawned. He leaned over to grab a cigarette from a pack on the floor, lit it, and turned back to me.

"What's this?" He touched the tattoo scrawled above my pubic bone. "'Too Tough to Die.'"

I told him about the rape, the open wound left by a zip knife when I'd been left for dead. No more details than if I'd been reporting the weather or a timetable. When I was done, he bent to kiss my shoulder.

"That must have been terrible."

I stared at the black square of window. From across the room his cell phone beeped. Quinn walked over and fumbled in his coat pocket. "Battery's almost dead. It's late. You hungry?"

"No. But probably I should eat."

"There's nothing here. I'll grab us some takeout from Aktu Taktu. Feel like coming?"

I shook my head. He dressed and grabbed his coat, opened the door, and stopped. "Lock this after me. No one's going to come by—but if someone does, don't let them in."

I pulled on my sweater, stood beside the window and watched as the car drove away, then drew the dead bolt. The cell tower's beacon did nothing to illuminate the ground below. If someone crept up to Quinn's place, I'd never know it. I remembered Anton's admonition that I buy a cell phone in Helsinki. Too late now.

I finished dressing and drank about half a gallon of water, trying to throw off the shaky sense that none of this was happening, that it was all a dream ignited by jet lag and booze and a photo taken in 1975. When I opened the bottle of Focalin, my hands trembled; I felt sweaty and sick. The face that gazed back at me from the kitchen mirror was as ravaged as Quinn's. I thought about his tattoos and wondered if murder had become instinctive for him, the way petty theft and lying were for me. I waited for my nausea to subside, then began to look around.

I didn't find much. A kitchen drawer contained pens, razor blades, matches, an expired driver's license, a ziplock bag of pot. In the bathroom were filthy towels, an overturned wastebasket, and a metal cabinet that contained several prescription bottles. The labels were in Icelandic; I didn't recognize the pills inside and decided against popping any. On the floor beside the toilet were old issues of *Record Collector* magazine and a paperback of *The Return of the King*.

It was the same copy Quinn reread obsessively in the 1970s, its cover a psychedelic mashup of mountains in flame and monsters in bruised colors. When I picked it up, it fell open to a page filled with sticklike letters. A runic alphabet. The margins held more runes in faded blue ballpoint. Quinn's name, I guessed, or maybe even mine, written decades ago.

I returned to the living room. A cheap particleboard chest of drawers held old band T-shirts and corduroy jeans, flannel shirts, a filmy red camisole, and several wadded-up thongs. I picked up the camisole, and a red passport fell out. The photo showed a blond woman, a few years younger but with the same pissed-off expression: Dagny Ahlstrand, born 15 March, 1960, resident of Uppsala.

I searched in vain for another passport or snapshots, notebook or spare set of keys—anything that might suggest a life other than the one conjured up by unwashed clothes and the empty bottles piled beneath the sink. I discovered nothing. No more alcohol, either, except for the Brennivín. I caved and drank some, chasing it with foul-smelling water, and went into the room where the LPs were stored.

It was like a meat locker in there: I could see my breath. I went from carton to carton, pulling out albums in hopes of finding some evidence of the Quinn I'd known.

At last I hit pay dirt. Beneath the room's sole window were two boxes, covered by a frayed plaid blanket. I recognized the blanket from Quinn's boyhood room in Kamensic, where he'd jammed it beneath the door when we were getting high. I pressed it against my face, breathing in dust and smoke, the faintest trace of jasmine incense, and settled on the floor, flipping through an alphabetized record of our shared adolescence. The Beatles, Chuck Berry, early Bowie; on through T. Rex and finally The Velvet Underground. I pulled out the original *White Light/White Heat* and tipped the glossy black album cover toward the overhead lamp. Under black light it revealed a skull, but now the ghostly sigil remained hidden. I pulled out the next album.

Spiky red letters spelled the word VIÐAR, the letter *I* an inverted cross. The minimalist cover photo showed a winter landscape: black spruce trees, a raven in flight above three young men wearing long black leather coats, black leather pants, high black boots. All tall and broad shouldered, their hair whipping around their shoulders. I've seen more cheerful faces in the Bellevue morgue. No corpse paint; just three piercing gazes that seemed to recognize me as an interloper in the northern wilderness. I held the album cover to the light, and sudden radiance leapt from the middle of the sleeve, igniting runic letters.

DOD SVART SOL

I realized then what it was: *Dead Black Sun,* the sole album by a Scandinavian band whose claim to fame, for me anyway, was that Ilkka Kaltunnen had shot their album cover, back in the early 1990s. That was long past the glory days of LPs, but bands still did vinyl pressings for the collector's market. I wondered why it was misfiled with Quinn's juvenilia. At least it was less embarrassing than *Frampton Comes Alive!*

Or maybe not—maybe this was the black metal equivalent of Gilbert O'Sullivan, and that's why he'd hidden it away. I removed the record from its sleeve, put it on the turntable, and sank into a chair to listen.

I expected shrieking guitars and jackhammer drums. Instead, horns echoed in a mournful fanfare that slowly died away into ominous silence, broken by an answering flourish of brazen trumpets that soared into a single, chilling note, held longer than I would have thought possible, before it, too, faded.

Gradually I became aware of the same note, even more plaintive and plucked repetitively on an acoustic guitar. Then a second guitar joined the first, and after a minute both were drowned out by two male voices, chanting. The vocals were buried too deep in the mix for me to understand them or even to tell if the words were

English or Norwegian. The effect should have been laughable, ersatz worshippers playing at a twentieth-century Black Mass.

Yet the voices, so raw and unpolished, had the opposite effect. One fell out of sync with the other, and I heard a sharp intake of breath, an unintelligible word sung off-key; and this conspired to make me feel as though I were listening to something that was in fact happening now, in this room, rather than fifteen years ago in a recording studio. The two voices grew louder, a litany abruptly silenced by the treble scream of an electric guitar. Beneath the razor chords echoed another sound—a third, guttural voice, grunting, and then a strident whine, like an engine in high gear. I drew my head beside the speaker, straining to hear.

For a fraction of a second it was unmistakable. Not a guitar or synthesizer, but an anguished scream. Almost immediately it was lost amid a cascade of drums and that same guttural voice, shouting hoarsely. The guitars rose to a deafening pitch as the voice faded. The song continued for another thirty seconds, ending in a cacophony of feedback, followed by a thunderclap.

Then silence.

I lifted the tonearm and stared at the record spinning soundlessly. Wind shook the walls; hail battered the lone window. At last I switched off the turntable and examined the album sleeve's back cover. No song titles. No band photo or production credits. Inside, only a blank paper jacket.

Nothing more. It seemed like a self-annihilating thing for an unknown band to do with their first album, but maybe that was the point.

I removed the LP from the turntable and held it to the light. In the old days, you'd sometimes find messages etched into the runout groove in the middle of a record, like "Do what thou wilt shall be the whole of the Law" inscribed on the original pressing of "Immigrant Song."

The groove on side one of *Dod Svart Sol* was smooth and glossy as though oil had been poured onto it. I turned the record over, tilting it back and forth until I saw it.

There was no bolt of radiance as in Ilkka's photographs; just a knot of coiled lines, fine as though etched with a sewing needle. I brought the disc closer to my eyes and lost the image, and after another minute's scrutiny, found it again. Half the size of a fingerprint, and almost as difficult to see: three skeletal arms, each with a bony hand that formed an interlocking pattern where it grasped a wrist. In the center of the image was a ghostly face created by the negative space left by the surrounding images.

The same symbol that was tattooed on Quinn's chest.

I stared until my eyes watered. What the hell was it? A record company logo? Then why would Quinn have it tattooed on his chest? I tried to remember what I knew about Viðar, other than the band's fleeting association with Ilkka. I came up with nothing. What had been their appeal for Quinn—or Ilkka? I could see how the brutal music might have attracted a Quinn numbed and hardened by prison. But Ilkka seemed far too coolly genteel, corked way too tight for adolescent satanic pyrotechnics.

Though I guessed that might have been the allure, if you were a smart, middle-class kid from the Helsinki suburbs, the kind of college student who got off on crime-scene photos. Maybe that whole dark, violent Oslo scene had shaped the teenage Ilkka the way the downtown New York scene had shaped me a million years ago. Until he grew out of it and got a life and career and family— everything he wanted, till someone snuffed him.

I started to put the album back on the turntable when I heard the sound of a car. Quickly I slid the LP back into its jacket. Halfway in, it stuck. I pulled it out and tried again, but the same thing happened.

Something else was inside. I edged my fingers into the opening and felt around till they closed on a thin piece of cardboard. I pulled it out: a lurid vintage postcard, the now-familiar greeting scrolled above a horned figure who dragged a sled that bore two weeping children bound with chains.

GRUSS VOM KRAMPUS!

I looked at the back of the card. It was blank.

Outside, the car's engine died. I pocketed the postcard, shoved the LP into its cover, returned it to the carton, and hurriedly draped the plaid blanket across it. I strode back into the living room just as Quinn stepped in, shaking rain from his coat.

"Dinner." He handed me a steaming bag. I sat on the bed and waited for him to join me. "Sorry it took so long. The place was hopping."

I didn't trust myself to speak, but Quinn didn't notice. We sat without talking and ate greasy burgers and reconstituted French fries stained red with paprika. When we were finished, Quinn smoked another cigarette, then threw his arm around me.

"You tired?"

"Not really."

"Good," he said, and pulled me down beside him.

16

Hours later Quinn's cell phone started beeping. Quinn slept through it, so I reached for it and stared blearily at a two-word text message.

help galdur

Looked like Baldur had gotten so wasted he'd misspelled his own name. I dropped the phone and dozed off till I was awakened again by a "Gimme Shelter" ringtone. This time I shoved the phone in Quinn's face. He looked at the time and sat up, groaning.

"Shit, it's after eight. I have to get back to the city; market's only open on weekends." He pointed to a counter. "Coffee's there."

I made coffee, went into the bathroom, and showered. When I walked back into the living room, Quinn grabbed me by the shoulder.

"What the fuck?" I tried to push him away.

"What were you doing in Helsinki?"

I stopped cold. "What do you mean?"

"What I just fucking said. What were you doing in Helsinki?"

"I told you—I was checking out some photos for Anton."

"What photos?" He shook me so hard my jaw snapped. "Whose fucking photos, Cass?"

"A guy. A photographer named Ilkka Kaltunnen." I glared at him, rubbing my jaw. "Don't hand me this shit, Quinn! You were the one who gave my name to Anton."

"Anton's dead."

"What?"

"I just talked to Baldur. They found Anton in a parking garage at the Helsinki airport. He'd been strangled. Someone shoved a candle in his eye."

"A candle? What the hell are you talking about?"

"You tell me." He pushed me against the wall. "Ilkka—what happened with him?"

"I don't know," I stammered. "Anton gave me an address. I got a cab to the place and talked to him. Ilkka Kaltunnen, the photographer. I hardly saw him. He showed me some photos he'd done. Anton was interested in buying them."

"What photos?"

"Bondage pictures." The lie came quick as breath. "Girls, a bunch of Asian girls, all trussed up. From Bangkok. Underage, probably, I didn't want to know too much."

Quinn held my eyes, then shoved me away. "Did you know Ilkka was dead when we got here last night?"

I wouldn't push my luck with another lie. "Yeah."

"Why didn't you tell me?"

"I don't know. It was all so . . . I mean, I just found you yesterday; everything happened so fucking fast. I just saw it on TV yesterday, in a bar here in Reykjavík."

"Did you tell Ilkka you knew me?"

"Why would I do that? I had no clue you knew him, or Anton. I couldn't pick Anton out of a police lineup."

"Well, now you won't have to." Quinn grabbed some clothes from the floor. "Baldur got a text message from Anton on Friday, the same message I just saw this morning. Baldur didn't text Anton back till last night. No answer. He tried calling Anton, still no answer. So he called a friend in Helsinki. The police are all over it."

"Fucking shit." No wonder Anton had misspelled Baldur's name. It was probably the last thing he did. "Are they . . . does anyone know about me?"

"I don't know. But Ilkka's place was ransacked. Bondage photos." He fixed me with a grim stare. "Why would Anton need you to look at bondage photos?"

"I don't know. I told him the deal was a go, far as I was concerned. I thought *he* killed Ilkka. Him or someone he hired, a hit man."

"The police say Anton was killed sometime Friday afternoon; they only found him in the parking garage yesterday. I doubt he was the killer—Anton liked to let other people do his dirty work for him." Quinn tossed me my leather jacket. "Let's go."

"Where?"

"Kolaportið. I don't know what the hell is going on, but I'm gonna act like nothing's wrong until I figure it out. You can check into a hotel or something and wait for me."

I threw the jacket back at him. "I'm not going anywhere. Anton owes me money; I don't have shit till he pays me."

"Then you better get used to shit, because Anton's not paying anyone anytime soon."

"You knew him. Ilkka."

I pulled the Krampus postcard from my pocket and held it up. Quinn stared at it, his deep-set eyes burning inside a skull mask. "Where did you get that?" he asked in a low voice.

"Tell me how you knew him."

He grabbed the postcard and threw it aside, then clamped a hand around my wrist. "Listen to me. You have to leave. There's an afternoon flight to New York. Change your return ticket; I'll drive you to the airport."

"I don't have a return ticket. And my credit card's tapped out."

"I'll pay for it."

"I told you, I can't go back to New York. I'm wanted for questioning about Kamestos already."

"Goddammit, Cass, this is fucked," Quinn shouted. "You have no idea how fucked! I don't know what you were doing with those guys, but this is some seriously bad shit. You're like a fucking bad penny, you know that? I was out of my fucking mind to go after you yesterday. I should've let Einar take care of you."

"You knew what was going on?"

I hauled back to punch him, but he pushed me away.

"No, of course I didn't know." He leaned against the wall and clutched his head. "I still don't know. And you know what? Don't fucking tell me, because I don't want to know. Bredahl's a sick Pekingese, and Ilkka—Ilkka's worse. I know he went straight and all that shit, but trust me, the guy used to sniff formaldehyde to get off. He's a fucking necrophile."

"Huh." I looked at him disdainfully. "Nice friends."

"Yeah, well, I know you, right?" He pounded the drywall. "I can't afford to get mixed up in this. There's too much old shit you don't know about. I could be deported, and if that happens, I'm fucked six ways from Sunday."

"Same with me."

"Yeah, but the difference is maybe no one here knows who you are, yet. Maybe no one gives a fuck. Or maybe not. But they know me. There's more people in Newark than in this whole country. Everyone knows everyone else. Everyone's related to everyone else. You can't hide, Cass."

"So I'll just lie low."

"Like you lay fucking low in Helsinki?"

"You seem able to disappear when you want."

"That's because I'm not a total fucking idiot, like some people I know. You're too old for this, Cass. I'm too old for it."

"Not too old to deal drugs."

"Who told you that?" He went into the storeroom and returned with a carton of vinyl. "It's more like a hobby. I'm trying to keep it that way. Look, Baldur just got a call from a guy who has some rare albums he wants to unload. He set up a meeting with the guy, but I can't trust Baldur with shit. He let go a Sun Records Elvis 45 once, worth five grand. So I have to get down there before I end up with a thousand dollars worth of crap. You can't stay here while I'm gone. And I'm not taking you with me to Kolaportið. I don't know what I'm going to do." He headed to the door. "I'll figure something out."

I got my stuff and followed him to the Jeep.

It was mid-morning and the air felt mild, almost springlike. Stars faded above a sea that paled from indigo to cobalt. By the time we hit the suburbs, sunlight flared along the distant mountaintops like grass fire. Neither of us had said a word. Quinn pulled the car into a church parking lot, ignoring the curious glances of people chatting nearby. He stared at a pair of gulls squabbling over a piece of trash. I dug into my bag for the Focalin, popped two, and held out the bottle. Quinn poured some pills into his palm and swallowed them, continuing to stare as the gulls tore apart a pizza box. I watched him uneasily from the corner of my eye. Finally he started the car and pulled back into the street.

"Where are we going?"

"Brynja's place." He didn't look at me. "Baldur's sister."

"Baldur told me she hates you."

"What, did you run a background check? She does hate me, I guess. But she loves her brother, and he's my business partner. She's got a gift shop; it's in a lousy location. She makes more money when she's at Kolaportið. But you probably won't run into anyone there. She's usually at the shop on Sunday doing accounts."

"You're not going to call first?"

"That'd just give her the chance to say no."

The shop was in a block of shabby little buildings with a view of distant snowcapped mountains, a dream of winter against the blue sky. There was an old gray Opel parked out front. Tattered flyers in the windows advertised Ayurvedic massage and elf tours. Brynja stood in the doorway, smoking a cigarette. She scowled when she saw the car pull up.

"Wait." Quinn opened the glove compartment, withdrew something, and turned to hand it to me. "I want you to take this."

I looked at him in disbelief. "Are you out of your fucking mind? I don't have enough problems, you want to give me a fucking gun?"

"Take it," he urged. I punched his arm.

"I'm not touching that. Put it away, damn it."

He glared at me, shoved the gun back into the glove compartment, and slammed it shut. "You know what your problem is, Cass? You can't think ahead. You're incapable of seeing three seconds into the future, unless there's a fucking bottle there." He turned to open his door. "Don't move."

He hopped out and hurried toward Brynja, greeted her perfunctorily, then began talking in a low voice. Brynja listened, her dark eyes fixed on me. Finally she shook her head. Quinn took her arm and bent his head to murmur into her ear. With a grimace she pulled away, threw the cigarette at the Opel, and stormed inside.

Quinn waved me over. "She says you can hang here for a couple hours."

"Yeah? What'd it cost you?"

"I told her I'd give Baldur the next two months off. With pay. I'll come back for you in a few hours."

"A few hours when?"

"I dunno. Let's say two o'clock. If I'm going to be late, I'll call Brynja."

"Then what?"

"I don't know." He stared across the housetops to the mountains. "Just wait for me. Whatever happens, don't leave. Got that? Do. Not. Leave. I'll figure something out."

He took my chin in his hand and gazed at me for a long moment, pulled me to him, and held me close.

"Cassie," he murmured. "You are a royal pain in my ass, you know that?"

He turned and walked to the car. I watched it pull away, dread tightening my gut, and went into the shop.

17

Brynja sat behind a counter, staring balefully at a computer register.

"I know this is some drug thing. Or more prostitutes. Lock the door." She looked up at me—a photographic negative of her brother, angry dark eyes and black hair, her lips a spiteful curve. She looked at least ten years older than Baldur, mid-thirties maybe. "Quinn is an evil man."

"Then why'd you let me in?"

"Better to watch the Devil than turn your back on him."

She glared as though she hoped to set my hair on fire. I ignored her, dropped my bag, and walked to the far side of the shop. Filthy windows tinted the midday sun a sour nicotine yellow. The room smelled of scorched coffee. Brynja's wares were a mix of Nordic trinkets and New Age cheese: refrigerator magnets featuring puffins and reindeer and trolls; postcards of geysers and improbably beautiful young people riding miniature blue-eyed horses; Viking key chains. Lots of rune jewelry, along with rune stones, rune cards, rune bottle openers, shot glasses, and coffee mugs. A one-stop shop for all your runic needs. I held up a sweatshirt emblazoned with a horned helmet and the words road to rune.

"Who the hell buys this stuff?"

"Americans." Brynja looked back at the computer screen. "And Japanese. The same people who go on the elf tours."

Brynja seemed happy to pretend I didn't exist, so I returned the favor and spent the next few hours wandering around the shop. There was a cabinet filled with books, including English titles like *Twilight of the Gods, Wisdom of the Runes,* and *Ásatrú for the Solitary Practitioner,* along with translations of various sagas and a bunch of maps showing where the elves lived, shrink-wrapped so I wouldn't drop in unannounced and without paying for directions. I flipped through a crudely illustrated, well-thumbed guide to sex with the hidden people, then stepped to another cabinet. This one held neat stacks of tea towels, red and white and green, brightly colored calendars, and a basket filled with Christmas ornaments. I picked up a kitschy figurine of a grinning, troll-like figure holding a spoon in each hand. He looked more like the Hamburglar than one of Santa's helpers, crudely painted and with a price tag that suggested the ornament was made of sterling silver rather than plastic. I dropped it and picked up a bearded troll peeking through a doorway. A hand-lettered sign above the basket read JÓLASVEINAR! YULE-BOYS! ICELANDIC SANTA CLAUS!

I stared at the leering troll: Door Slammer. The other one would be Spoon Licker. I dug through the basket and withdrew a troll gnawing a candle as though it were a turkey drumstick. I thought of Suri, her spine severed by a slammed door; Anton with a candle jammed into his eye socket. And Ilkka . . .

I searched until I found a figurine who wore a bowl on his head, like a hat.

"Shit," I whispered.

"I know. They're ridiculous." Brynja watched me, her expression resigned. "Santa Claus has conquered Iceland."

"You sell a lot of these?"

"I don't sell a lot of anything anymore."

"But these are popular?"

"Oh sure." She looked away. "Too popular. Two hundred years ago they were a black story for a winter night. Now they are Santa Claus," she said in disgust. "Everything that belonged to us has been destroyed so that someone else can get rich."

"I hear you." I turned the ornament over: made in china. "But you're making money on this crap."

"Once. Now there is barely any money. I don't know what will happen to me. To all of us."

I dropped the ornament into the basket. "What about your brother?"

"He's young. He'll move to someplace warm. That's what all the young people are doing. We have different mothers; Baldur's mother lives in Madrid. He'll probably go there and start over."

"As a record dealer?"

Brynja's mouth grew tight. "He has a degree in engineering. If he hadn't met Quinn, my brother would be far away by now."

"What, did Quinn pull him from a blazing car wreck? Seems like Baldur could leave whenever he wants to. Maybe he likes working with Quinn. Maybe the money's good."

"The money is shit."

She stood and walked to a counter holding a coffeemaker and several mugs. She poured herself a cup and stared at me, her eyes chips of smoky glass.

"Baldur got into trouble with drugs." She sipped her coffee.

"Not using them; selling them."

"For Quinn?"

"And others. The police didn't catch him, but . . . Quinn had to pay off some of my brother's debts. Now Baldur does favors for him."

I imagined what kind of favors Quinn might call in. "Does Baldur know a guy named Anton?"

Brynja said nothing. "From Oslo," I went on. "Norwegian guy."

"No," she said. "I know people there. From a long time ago. Quinn does, too. But not Baldur."

I was starting to wonder how it was that Brynja knew so much about a guy she hated. I casually examined an ID bracelet etched with runes. "Was that before you and Quinn hooked up?"

Silence; then a terse "Yes. A long time ago."

Bingo. I waited for her to go on. After a moment she asked, somewhat warily, "He told you about us?"

"Not how you broke up." I shrugged. "Forget it. He's an asshole."

"He is worse than an asshole."

Brynja reached behind the coffeemaker and withdrew a bottle of Brennivín. She poured a slug into her coffee, handed me the bottle. I sloshed a few inches into a mug with a volcano motif. Brynja drank, poured herself another few inches of Brennivín, and fixed me with an icy stare.

"Him and his friends. They are evil men, all those Odinists."

"What?"

"Odinists." She looked at me suspiciously. "I thought you knew Anton."

I downed the rest of my Brennivín. I knew Odin was a Norse god, but his details were fuzzy. "I never really hung out with Anton much. Or those other guys." I hesitated, then added, "Just Ilkka."

"Ilkka." Her tone grew wistful. "I almost forgot about Ilkka. What happened to him, do you know? He disappeared after he stopped doing the magazine work."

"I think he got married. And had kids. I saw him a little while back."

"He was so smart. I never understood why he got involved with that scene." She stared into her mug. "We were all young and stupid."

Brynja didn't look stupid now; just drunk. Me, I drink to remember. If the right music's playing, if it's dark enough and I'm loaded, I can sometimes catch a flicker of that 3:00 a.m. feeling I used to live for. Brynja, though, was drinking to forget.

And it looked like she'd get lucky real soon, which meant I'd have a hard time getting anything useful out of her. I poured what remained of the Brennivín into my mug. She didn't seem to notice. She began to straighten a stack of postcards, folded the road to rune sweatshirt, and walked to the next counter, where she paused in front of a display of black leather wristbands, ornamented with spikes and round silver bosses.

"Look at these." Her voice slurred. "Baldur told me these would sell, but no one wants them. Kids from Oslo and Bergen maybe, but not Reykjavík."

I walked over and picked up one of the wristbands. It was a nice piece of hardware, thick black leather, steel spikes sharp as thorns. Brynja took it from my hand and undid the clasp, put it around my wrist, and loosely fastened it.

"There." She raised her hand with the pinkie and thumb extended—devil horns.

I made a fist. "This thing's heavy."

"Yes, for heavy metal." She laughed too hard, steadying herself against the counter. I tightened the wristband a notch, then stopped.

Beside the clasp was an engraved silver disc. I turned to the window, squinting until I made out the design—a triskele formed of three skeletal, grasping hands.

"It cost extra to have them engraved," said Brynja. "I had to order them special. I should make Baldur pay for them."

I ran my finger over the silver boss. "What's this mean, this design with the hands?"

"That is the Gripping Beast. It's a very old symbol, from the Broa burial on Gotland in Sweden." She picked up another wristband, spikes bristling. "A Viking symbol."

I pointed at the sweatshirt she'd just folded. "Like the helmet."

"Perhaps. Only these are more..." She paused. "Cultic."

"Right." I made the devil sign. It looked far more impressive with the wristband on. "You'd make a killing with these at Ozzfest."

"No. I mean a true cult. A religion. We all used to wear them. It is a symbol of the past's hold upon the present and the future. This in the middle..."

She touched the spectral face formed by the interlocking hands. "That is Death. Some say it is the face of Odin, who gained power over death by being slain and then reborn; but I do not believe that. Nothing is more powerful than Death. It reaches from the past to destroy us, yet no future world can exist without it. Every step you take is across a bridge that will end in that country. This design..."

She turned the wristband so its spines caught the pallid sunlight. "Now it is very common; you see variants in many places, just like all the spikes and leather. You can buy them online. But fifteen years ago, it was harder to find them. And we didn't have much money; we had to make them ourselves, from old belts and nails. It was Anton's idea. He wanted to sell them at Forsvar, his club, and then after Helvete closed, he was going to open his own black metal store. Even then, all Anton wanted was money."

She dropped the wristband as though it were something foul and looked at me. "I threw mine into the ocean on the ferry crossing back from Kiel. You never had one?"

"No. Like I said, I didn't hang out that much with them." Whoever *them* was. I mustered an offhand tone. "And Ilkka wasn't really into it."

"Yes he was," retorted Brynja. "In the beginning, he was the biggest one. He started everything, after he came to Norway: He was so in love with the idea of resurrecting an ancient religion, of making it all new. Creating new rituals, modern rituals...Ilkka was in love with it because it was not his own history as a Finn. The way Americans fall in love with another place or a lost part of their history. Do you understand?

"And he was so brilliant. The others were just boys—kids. I was only seventeen. I left home and followed a boy to Oslo. He was in a band, and I wanted to escape from Iceland. I was so stupid; all I cared about was Halmar. Did you know him? He was very cute then; he had long blond hair and was very sweet, trying to look tough. He's fat now; you wouldn't recognize him. He works in social services here in Reykjavík. But he broke my heart. That's why I started seeing Quinn, to make him jealous."

"Did it work?"

"No." She laughed. "Quinn was too old. Everyone thought he was creepy—a cradle robber, because I was so young. But he always had coke, you know? Ecstasy, everything. He was a drug dealer; he'd been in prison. I thought that was so great. He was like a gangster. And we never had gangsters in Reykjavík. Or Oslo. Just a bunch of stupid boys burning down churches. They were all so angry, because they were so bored. They had more time to be bored afterward, in prison."

She stared out the window. I handed her my mug, still half full; she nodded and drank as we watched the sun dip behind the Lego-land rooftops. When she looked at me again, her eyes were red, as though she'd been trying to see an impossible distance.

"Quinn said you were an old friend from New York. Have you been in prison, too?"

"Not yet."

Darkness overtook the room around us as another hour slowly passed, shadows roosting in corners and ceiling and pooling across the floor. I waited for Brynja to turn on a lamp, but she remained motionless beside me, the mug held tight to her breast. The last light leaked from the sky. A star glimmered into view and faded so quickly I wondered if I had imagined it. After a long time I spoke.

"Do you know a band called Viðar?" Brynja inhaled sharply. "That symbol," I went on, "I've seen it before. On a record by them."

"I told you, it's not unusual. Maybe in America, but not in Scandinavia."

She answered too quickly, set her empty mug on the counter, and turned to me, her face a dark blur, as though it were my own face half glimpsed in a mirror. "Who are you?"

"I told you. Quinn's friend."

"You didn't tell me that. He did. You're lying. You were not in Oslo then, or you would have known that the name is pronounced *Vithar*, not *Vidar*. Even a stupid American would have remembered that. You come from nowhere, but even Quinn is afraid of you. Tell me who you really are."

She drew her head close to mine. I smelled raw alcohol on her breath, and a foul scent like an abscessed tooth.

"You're crazy. Why would Quinn be scared of me?"

"I will tell you," she whispered. "Because you carry the dead with you. On your skin—I can smell them."

She dug her nails into my palm. "'On all sides she gathers hordes of the dead, back bent to bear them homeward to Hell. Shield-maiden, skull-heavy.' That is you."

She really was crazy. I kicked her and she fell back, clutching her leg.

I grabbed my bag and ran to the door. The room erupted with light, a blaze that immediately subsided. Headlights. I peered out the window, hoping for Quinn's Cherokee. Instead I saw a Volvo wagon. A stocky figure stepped around it and hurried toward the door. I yanked it open before he could knock.

"*Takk.*" A balding man stepped into the room, gray faced and out of breath. He flicked a light switch, frowning when he saw Brynja doubled over.

"She flipped out," I explained. "Who are you?"

"I'm Magnus—a friend of Baldur's." He looked more puzzled to see me than anything else. "Yes, she has fits sometimes. Mostly when she drinks. Is Baldur here?"

I shook my head. Brynja got to her feet and hobbled across the room. She shot me a hateful look before turning to Magnus. "I spoke to him this morning, he was going to make sure Svana got there to watch my stall. I had to do accounts."

"Svana was there; I spoke to her," said Magnus. "She said Baldur never showed up, and she was there very early. I had money for him, that's why I was starting to worry. It's not like him to forget about money."

"What about Quinn?" I broke in.

Magnus shrugged. "No, he wasn't there either. No one unpacked anything; their tables were empty. Baldur's car was in the lot; it's still there, with everything locked inside. I didn't see Quinn's Jeep, though. I keep calling Baldur, but he's not answering his mobile."

"Quinn dropped me off this morning," I said. "He told me he was going to the market. He was supposed to come back and get me by two. He said he'd call if he was late, but he never did."

"He didn't answer his cell phone, either." Magnus opened the door to an adjoining room and peered in, as though he suspected someone of hiding there. "Huh."

"I told you, he's not here." Brynja limped over and angrily shut the door. "Have you called Astridur?"

"Yes. She hadn't heard from him either. She was upset because they were supposed to meet for lunch. He never showed up." Magnus's brow furrowed. "That's just not like Baldur, especially with Astridur. You're sure he didn't call you?"

"No one called. No one has been here. Except for her." Brynja glared at me. "Please take her with you when you go."

"I can't." Magnus headed for the door. "I'm bringing the children to my mother's for dinner. If you hear from Baldur, tell him to call me."

"Hey!" I chased him outside. "I'm not staying here. She's a fucking nutjob. And she's tanked. I have to talk to Quinn. Take me with you, I'll help you find him."

"I can't do that. I'm sorry." Magnus hopped into the Volvo. "Make her drink some coffee. If Baldur shows up, tell him to call me."

I shouted after him, but he just gunned the motor and drove off. It had started to snow, fine flakes that glowed crimson in the Volvo's taillights. I stood in the cold and watched until it was out of sight, then returned inside.

18

Brynja was bowed over the sink with the water running. After a minute she turned the water off and looked at me, her face flushed and wet.

"I feel better now." She picked up a Yuleboy dish towel and dried her face on it, then bent to inspect her leg. "You attacked me. I should call the police."

"Be my guest. It was self-defense. Look, do you have any idea where Quinn could be? He said he'd be back by two and that was, what? Three hours ago?"

Brynja looked at me with contempt. "You think Quinn is reliable?"

"No, but . . ."

She walked back to a closet and removed her coat and several bags. "I'm going home."

"So, what—I wait here? Can't you even call him? Can I?"

"I should never have let you in here. You or Quinn. Here—" She thrust a cell phone at me angrily.

"Do you know his number?"

"I do not."

"Neither do I. Forget it."

She started to pull on her coat. "You can walk from here; maybe he will find you in the dark. I'm leaving."

"Look," I said, hoping I didn't sound as desperate as I felt. "I was always jealous of you and Quinn, that's all. I wanted to know what was going on with you guys back then, and he would never tell me. He asked me to come here to Reykjavík. Now I'm here and I find out you're here, too. I didn't know whether you guys were still involved."

It sounded half plausible, even to me. But I could see by Brynja's sour face that she wasn't easily placated. I pointed at the volumes of New Age wackery, hoping to distract her. "So what was that before? Some kind of Icelandic curse?"

"A curse?" she sneered. "No. That is from the *Völuspá*, one of the Eddic poems. In Iceland we grow up reading them."

I grew up reading *Hägar the Horrible*, but didn't mention that.

"It's the prophecy of the Völva," Brynja went on. "A wisewoman—a seer. But all she sees is ruin and the end of things. Fimbulwinter. Ragnarök."

She stopped and stared at me, brooding. "You see things, too. Terrible things. Dead things."

My skin went cold, and I looked away. "A prophecy. Is that what the cult was based on? With your friends in Oslo?"

"Ilkka's friends were all involved in a revival of the old Norse religions. The boys in the black metal scene came from the suburbs, nice families, but they hated all that. They hated many things, but most of all Christianity. They believed the priests had destroyed the heathen religion—the true religion for the people of the north. And of course that is true. So they loved anything anti-Christian. Some played at being Satanists, like Emperor and Fenriz. Now most of them see it is ridiculous. They have become adults.

"But some, once they outgrew the Devil, they became devoted heathens. In Iceland that tradition remains close to us through our literature. That's what Ilkka studied at university. He was a Finn, but he was obsessed with the sagas, Norse folklore and archaeology and anthropology. He was in love with old things. Dead things, like the Danish bog people who were strangled and thrown into the mire a thousand years ago. He was obsessed with finding connections between all the old northern European beliefs; he thought they could be revived. And even though he was a Finn living in Norway, he believed that the purest form of these beliefs would be found in Iceland. Because we are so isolated. Our language is the closest to Old Norse. We practiced our pagan religion longer than in Europe. And Ásatrú, modern heathenism, began here in the 1970s."

"Those churches that burned down—did Ilkka do that? Was that your friends?"

She wouldn't meet my eyes. "I don't know. I was gone by then. All those black metal guys hanging out at the Elm Street Café? None of them ever laughed, except for Quinn. I finally couldn't stand it, so I came back here. In Iceland, no one cares if you are anti-Christian. Live and let live. But in Norway and Sweden, more groups formed. Ásatrú, Odinism. They read the sagas and Eddas, like Christians read the Bible. They follow the old gods. Many of them practice in secret, but they are real."

"What do you mean, 'real'? This is, like, a religion inspired by 'Immigrant Song.'" I gestured at the posters for elf tours, the piles of plastic trolls and rune stones. "I know you sell all this to tourists. But you can't believe in this Viking stuff."

Brynja scowled. "Americans—all you ever want to talk about is elves and Vikings. And Björk. You don't even know what *Viking* means. They are only the men who went to sea, the raiders. The heathen religions are much older than that. It is in our blood, whether or not you believe in it. And it doesn't matter what I believe. Christ is real for Christians, yes? And what is not real, some believers will try to make it real. There may be no Satan, but the people who burned those churches and murdered were doing his work all the same.

"Scandinavia is not like America, and Iceland is the safest place in the world. We still have few murders. But the Internet has changed everything. And immigration, and now the bank crash—people have become angry. But in those days, violence was like a drug we weren't used to. People fell in love with it—with hatred and death, darkness. Because there is a beauty there, too, in the darkness. The northern sky—the total emptiness. You cannot imagine it. You stand on top of a glacier like Vatnajökull at midnight in the winter—you will see how your life is worth nothing, compared to that. And some people, they see that emptiness and need to fill it up with even greater darkness."

"Is that what you wanted?"

"For a little while. Until I saw what was inside that darkness."

I recalled what Suri had told me about Anton Bredahl. *He had a bouncer at that club, a really scary guy. . . . He was with his girlfriend one night, and she was carrying a bag, and there was a head in it.*

"What did Quinn do when he was in Oslo?" Brynja didn't reply. "When you met him—did he have a job?"

"He worked at Forsvar," she said at last. "Anton's club. He was the bouncer there."

"What do you mean?" I grabbed her but she shook me off.

"What do you mean, he—"

She walked to the register to retrieve her coat. "I'm going to Baldur's. We'll see if Quinn is there. You can ask him all these questions. Ask him about Jens Ramstad. And Ellisabet Anders, and all the other 'work' he did for Anton. Ask him why he cannot leave Iceland."

"But—"

"I need you to go now."

In the Opel, Brynja refused to speak; she just stared straight ahead as we drove across town. I clutched my bag and tried to stay calm, tugging at my sleeve: The wristband's spikes had torn the jacket's lining. I fought the urge to grab the wheel and drive blindly away from here, to—

Where? Toy city that it was, Reykjavík was unreadable to me. The grid of crosshatched streets seemed at once small yet infinitely complex, like a computer chip. Those distant, ominous mountains faded in and out of view as though some giant hand continually adjusted a vast gray monitor. I'd always assumed agoraphobics simply felt unnaturally attached to their cramped rooms, but now I realized what it must be like to sense the sky waiting outside the door, ready to crush you like a monstrous fist.

Fine snow flowed like smoke around the steady traffic. I couldn't see much besides the ghostly lights of apartment buildings. Black-clad figures straggled along the sidewalk, heads bowed as though the approaching headlights would burn them. My head thrummed from the Brennivín. The Focalin buzz had long faded, replaced by dread that burned into my veins like quicklime and the same atavistic horror that fueled my night terrors.

But I was awake now. The poison inside me came from the world outside: people who wouldn't meet my eyes; withered trees; that cancerous, enveloping darkness. I fumbled in my bag for a bottle that wasn't there; fought a wave of nausea I knew was the precursor to blacking out. I cracked my window to let in a rush of cold air and forced myself to breathe deeply. Then I pushed up my sleeves and jabbed the spiked wristband against the inside of my arm until my eyes watered and I dropped my hand with a gasp.

"Close the window," said Brynja. She reached to turn up the heat. "We'll be there soon."

The traffic had slowed; a line of crimson taillights crept ahead of us. It wasn't snowing that hard; I would have thought that drivers here wouldn't be put off by the weather. Brynja muttered to herself, then turned on the radio to a news station.

After a few minutes the bottleneck eased and we could see what had caused the slowdown. Several vehicles had pulled to the side of the road, including a police car. Two cops stood in the snow, talking to a small group of people.

Brynja frowned. The Opel slowed almost to a halt; the car behind us honked. Brynja tapped the accelerator and drove another fifty feet before turning down a road that led to a small apartment complex. A single streetlamp threw sulfur-colored light across drifted snow and a row of parked vehicles. Brynja's mouth tightened as a police cruiser raced down the drive past us.

People were clustered beneath the apartment's concrete awning, faces glowing blue as they held up cell phones to take pictures. Brynja slammed on the brakes. The Opel came to a stop. She jumped out and ran to where the cruiser had parked, its high beams spotlighting the ground beneath a straggly evergreen. I leaned over to turn off the engine, pocketed the keys, and followed her. A moment later she began to scream.

19

I started after Brynja, thought better of it, and instead walked up the embankment that led back to the main road, where I had a better view of the parking lot. A figure sprawled beneath the evergreen, his hair a blaze of silver in the cruiser's headlights. A shadow seemed to obscure his face. Then I realized that *was* his face, collapsed like a rotting jack-o'-lantern. I quickly retraced my steps.

More cruisers pulled into the lot. Brynja's screams were swallowed by the blast of a police bullhorn. A cop restrained her as she fought to get to Baldur's corpse; she pummeled the cop, and a policewoman hurried to pull her away. Lights appeared in apartment windows, and more people began to emerge from the building's back door. Several cars had pulled onto the side of the main road to rubberneck. A tall man stood beside an older Range Rover, staring at the scene below, the collar of his overcoat turned up against the snow and something cradled against his chest. He seemed to be breathing heavily. When he turned to get into his vehicle, I saw it was the guy who'd chased me—Einar Broddursson.

I glanced back but couldn't find Brynja in the crowd of cops and onlookers. I hurried to the Opel, started it, and drove back up to the main road. An ambulance wailed past, racing toward the apartment complex, and another police car.

In all the confusion, no one stopped me or the Range Rover a few car-lengths ahead. I remembered that repeated refrain: There are few murders in Iceland. I could only assume that nobody on the Reykjavík police force wanted to miss this one.

Traffic moved slow and tight, which made it easier to keep track of Einar. Sleet crackled like sugar glass beneath the Opel's studded tires; more than once the car began to slide. I don't spend a lot of time behind the wheel, and stealing a car belonging to someone whose brother had just been murdered probably wasn't the best way to ease myself back into crosstown traffic, especially on ice-covered roads in a place where the sun only shines for fifteen minutes a day.

Not to mention the onset of alcohol- and light-deprived psychosis that made me feel as though ants were tunneling into my skull. I knew the signs and I knew the cure. When the going gets tough, the tough get fucked up. I kept hold of the wheel with one hand and dug inside the slit in my jacket until I found the Baggie I'd hidden back in New York.

The Range Rover was a block ahead of me. We were somewhere near the water. From the corner of my eye I saw black sky unrolling above thickets of steel masts. There were fewer cars here, so when the Range Rover slowed, I did the same, letting a truck pull between us in case Einar had noticed me tailing him. I cupped the little glassine envelope in my palm, opened it, and tipped a tiny blast onto the back of my hand; snorted it, then shoved the envelope into my jeans pocket. By now the Opel had drifted into the other lane. I yanked the wheel and hit the wipers, smearing slush and grit across the windshield until I picked out the Range Rover's taillights through the sleet.

The crystal engulfed my brain like sunrise over an ice floe. Phil was right: This was the stuff. My exhaustion vanished; my eyes could pierce the dark like lasers. The first rush of crank is like a miracle from God: You can't believe you can feel this great and still be alive. Of course, a lot of times you're not alive for very long. You have to pace yourself, which is hard to remember when your neurons are moving so fast you can see them dancing in front of your eyes. The trick is to have a goal, something to think about besides doing another line. The difficulty is finding a potentially useful goal. I once spent two days playing Crazy Eights with a bassist and another twelve hours fucking him. Neither of us ever got off, and we might still be doing it if the lead singer hadn't broken the door down and sucker punched his bandmate.

At the moment, here in Reykjavík, I wasn't quite that far gone; just wasted enough to think that following a guy I didn't know down a side road that looked like it'd been firebombed was a good idea. I skirted potholes bigger than apartments I've crashed in. Unfinished construction lined both sides of the street, squat duplexes that looked as though they'd been designed by the winner of the Best Gulag-Inspired Architecture Contest. There were no streetlights, no lights in any of the buildings; just graffiti scrawled on an enormous concrete culvert that, judging from tracks in the slush and a pyramid of cigarette butts, had been recently used as a half-pipe by skate kids. At least someone in Reykjavík was having fun.

About three blocks ahead of me, the Range Rover came to a stop, right before the street ended in a tangle of construction equipment. I swung the Opel down the next side street and turned off the ignition. My entire body shook—adrenaline on top of crystal meth: a cardiac-arrest cocktail. Some booze would have calmed me down, and I did a fast recon of the Opel, hoping Brynja might have stored some Brennivín under the seat.

Unless it was in the wheel well, I was out of luck. I considered hanging on to the keys, but decided I'd risk going on foot. If and when the Reykjavík cops got over their excitement at having a real-life murder victim, they'd start looking for the Opel. I wiped the wheel and keys with my scarf and dropped the keys on the seat. Maybe I'd get lucky and one of the skate kids would make off with the car.

I slung my bag over my shoulder and stepped outside. Sleet lanced my face as my hair froze into a brittle helmet. God knows where I'd left my watch cap. The crank made me sweat, so the cold felt nice; a bad sign, but I was too hyped to care. I walked past empty duplexes and piles of black tephra gravel, treacherous going with the icy pavement underfoot, until I reached the block where the Range Rover was parked in front of the last unit.

These houses looked like they'd been built before the money ran out. There were windows, even if most were broken, and the buildings had doors and bright red sheet-metal roofs. Einar's vehicle was the only car, though two bicycles leaned against the front stoop. The duplex had a good view of a chain-link fence, beyond which stretched a vacant lot where a forest-green excavator gleamed like a Tonka toy that had just been unwrapped.

I stared at the duplex. Its windows glowed faintly with parchment-colored light, and I heard the throb of bass-heavy music.

A broken window had been patched with plywood. A shadow moved across another window, and I crouched behind the Range Rover, expecting Einar to materialize with a tire iron. Instead a woman shouted angrily, her voice immediately drowned by music loud enough to make the door shake. After a minute I straightened and peered through the Range Rover's passenger window.

Inside was a frozen blur. I scratched the ice with my fingernails, then used the spiked wristband to splinter it so I could see the car's interior. It was empty except for some oversize magazines strewn across the backseat.

Only they weren't magazines. I saw a flare like Saint Elmo's fire erupting from a spoon jammed into a man's tongueless mouth, and beneath this, the corner of another print.

"Fuck me," I said.

Ilkka's photos.

I yanked at the car door. It was frozen shut. I banged my fist against it, glancing at the house. The music thumped on and nothing moved inside, so I hammered at the door until the frozen latch gave way. I scrambled into the backseat. I pushed the photos aside so I wouldn't drip on them, yanked a T-shirt from my bag, then flattened each print on the seat beside me.

They were badly creased, and a corner had been torn from Svellabrjótur, the man beneath the ice. Worse was a long tear in the photo of the girl in the blizzard, like lightning splitting the sky. Photoshop would make it disappear.

But as an investment, a one-of-a-kind original monoprint, the photo was ruined. They all were. I remembered Ilkka's eerie calm as he peeled the protective tissue from each one; the rapture that filled his face as his masterworks were revealed for the first time to another pair of eyes.

All that malign, beautiful light had been extinguished, and Il-kka with it. If I'd stayed to have dinner with him in Helsinki, I'd probably be dead myself. But I might have learned the secret of those photos.

I stared through the car window at a street glazed black with ice, the rows of shoddy, half-constructed buildings left to collapse beneath the weight of winter and neglect. Whoever wanted these prints had killed three, maybe four, people to get them, then treated the photos like junk mail. They were worthless now to any collec-tor.

But not to me. I grabbed the photos and began to roll them into a tube, when I realized something was wrong.

There weren't five photos, but six. I shuffled through them again, trying to remember the bizarre litany of names: Door Slam-mer, Icebreaker, Window Peeper, Spoon Licker, Meat Hook.

And one other. Unlike the rest, it was an interior shot, taken in a darkened room with a wide-angle lens. No windows or lights of any kind. Somehow he'd positioned his camera so that it captured a faint gleam reflected in a fragment of broken glass, a beer bottle, an ashtray where a cigarette still burned.

And eyes. Like the bright pinpoints of rodents trapped in a root cellar—only these weren't rats but people standing in a loose semicircle, their bodies almost indistinguishable from the sur-rounding darkness. I could discern the dim outlines of legs and arm, and the curve of a hand cupping a match that illuminated the face above it—a heavyset man with thinning hair and a high fore-head, the only figure that might be recognizable to someone who knew him.

Even though I'd never seen him, I knew I was looking at An-ton Bredahl. It had to be him: That was why he was so intent on acquiring all six photos. Maybe he thought Ilkka had destroyed it, but here was the proof he hadn't.

I counted the figures—five. Ilkka would be elsewhere in the room, behind his Speed Graphic. It was a camera you could use for blackout photography: Just replace the ordinary bulb with one that had been coated inside with a special lacquer that would block out all visible rays and only transmit infrared. You'd need a slow shutter speed, like 1/30, and a wide lens.

And your subject would have to be within close range.

I looked closer and saw that there seemed to be a seventh person in the center of the group, head bowed or turned away so that the eyes weren't visible. When I squinted, I realized what the seventh figure was: an inverted body, suspended from the ceiling by thick chains that I'd mistaken for metal posts. On the floor beneath was a dark object, a bowl or basin.

I swore, rolled the photo into a narrow tube, and stuffed it into the lining of my jacket. I did the same to the others, wrapping them in a spare T-shirt, and stuffed this bulky cylinder into my bag, beneath the Konica. Then I sat and tried to get my shit together.

Snorting crank isn't like snorting coke. You don't get that volcanic rush followed by a crash that sends you running for the next line. It's more a steady pulse of electricity. You're like one of those corpses hooked up to a battery and galvanized into motion. My heart felt like it was trying to punch through my rib cage. I couldn't have slept if my life depended on it, though at this point it didn't seem like my life depended on much.

I looked at the car window and saw a disembodied arm hanging there, fingertips glittering with crystallized blood. I bolted upright. The arm was gone.

I didn't think I'd done enough crank to get spun, but maybe I should have factored in the general atmosphere of being in a country that looked like the set for a zombie remake of the Shackleton voyage. Nothing was going to make me feel any better, except maybe being able to make someone else feel worse.

I needed a weapon. The glove compartment held only a stash of Icelandic candy bars and documents that identified Einar Broddursson as the Range Rover's owner. I pocketed the candy bars and retrieved the crank. I guessed Einar had about six inches on me and another sixty pounds. I'd be crazy going up against him, but that was how the berserkers did it, right? I scooped some crystals into my pinkie nail and snorted them. I could smell my own sweat— bleach cut with grain alcohol. Eyes streaming, I grabbed my bag, stumbled out, and walked to the back of the car.

There was still no sign that anyone in the house had noticed me. The sleet had changed back to snow. The rear door's latch was frozen, so I stepped back and kicked it. The door popped open, and I pulled up the floor liner. There was a large sandbag in the storage area beneath, jumper cables, and a rusted shovel. I grabbed the shovel and headed for the front door of the house.

Inside it was dim and sounded like a battle of the bands where both groups had taken the stage at the same time. The amplified screech of guitars barely held its own against some kind of percolating electronica. I followed the electronica to where candlelight seeped from an open doorway, and stepped inside. Someone screamed, and I saw a figure scramble into the shadows cast by a row of flickering votive candles. There was a narrow bed, a beanbag chair, and a laptop on the floor, opened to a Facebook page.

The music continued to bubble from a tiny speaker beside the laptop. I strode over and stomped on it. The room immediately grew quiet enough that I could hear panting. I grabbed one of the votive candles and traced the sound to a teenage girl cowering against the wall, clutching a blanket. She stared at me, terrified, and babbled incomprehensibly until I ordered her to shut up.

"Where's Einar?"

She shook her head. I slammed the shovel into the wall so hard the point got stuck in the bare Sheetrock. The girl squealed and gestured toward the hall. I handed her the votive candle, extracted the shovel, and kicked through a litter of shattered plastic back into the corridor. Behind me I heard the front door slam. *Run, rabbit, run,* I thought.

With the electronica silenced, there was only the blare of some kind of grindcore. I hoisted the shovel and walked toward a glow at the end of the corridor. Tiptoeing was hardly necessary: The chain-saw Muzak made the walls shake. I passed a room filled with cardboard boxes, furniture, rolled-up rugs, lamps. Tarps were nailed across unfinished windows; bare wires poked from the walls. The air smelled of mildew and rotten eggs.

But it was still a lot cleaner than any squat I'd ever seen. And it was warm, which made me think that whoever lived here must've figured out a way to tap into the geothermal grid.

Abruptly the clanging music fell silent. I stopped, held my breath, and heard a woman's querulous voice; then a man's, reedier than I'd expected from a guy Einar's size. He sounded pissed off. The music roared back on, then off, then on. I headed for the kitchen and halted just outside the door.

Einar and a buxom, well-coiffed blond woman sat at a table with the remains of a take-out pizza, a bottle of vodka, and an iPod, screaming at each other. Plywood had been nailed across the room's sole window, but someone had tacked a brightly colored piece of fabric onto it, and a matching rug covered the concrete floor. Coats hung from the wall—Einar's loden-green overcoat; a black anorak; a cotton-candy-pink fake-fur jacket. A laptop and a stack of papers had been shoved into a corner beside a set of iPod speakers.

It was like some weird diorama of twenty-first-century domestic life, illuminated by a conical, battery-powered Ikea lantern: *Homeless Middle-Class Couple Arguing Over the iPod.* I waited till the music rose to a deafening pitch, then walked over and kicked the chair out from under Einar. He hit the floor, bellowing. I grabbed the battery lamp and shone it in the woman's face.

"Get out of here," I said.

Her face twisted as she swung at me but missed. I clocked her with the shovel's handle, and she dropped like a stunned grizzly. The room fell silent as the iPod skidded across the floor. Einar cried out, bending over her, then turned to me, his face white.

"You killed Gilda!"

I nudged her with my boot. "She's not dead."

He shouted and lunged at me, and I decked him with the shovel. He fell, groaning. I waited for him to catch his breath, then prodded him with the shovel's blade.

"Where'd you get those photos?" He stared at me blankly. "Where's Quinn?"

"Who?"

"Don't you fuck with me." I swung the shovel across the table, scattering plastic glasses and plates. "What did you do with Quinn?"

"Nothing! I haven't seen him."

"Like you haven't seen Baldur? Or Ilkka? Who are you?"

"Einar. Einar Broddursson." He raised a hand imploringly. "I'm sorry, you're in the wrong house. We have no drugs here, no money—"

"I don't care about your goddamn house. I'm looking for Quinn O'Boyle. Since you just killed his partner, I figured you might know where he is."

"Quinn? What are you talking about?" The reedy voice cracked. "I didn't kill Baldur! Fucking shit—"

He started to bolt. I kicked him and he reeled against the wall. I drew the shovel's blade to within an inch of his throat.

"I saw you at Baldur's apartment. I went inside your car; I found the photos. I know where they came from; I know who took them. Don't lie to me; I was fucking *there*. Now tell me where Quinn is."

"I don't know. It's true! I swear it. I drove by, I saw the accident and recognized Baldur, that's all. Just like you, if you stopped to watch." He stared at the door behind me, his eyes widening. "Where's my daughter? If you hurt her, I'll—"

"If you want to keep being her daddy, you better answer me. Inside the flea market—I saw you watching me, and then you came after me with a gun."

"A gun?"

"Or something. You were reaching into your pocket."

"I was reaching for my fucking mobile." He looked incredulous. "I saw that Quinn was gone; I thought I would help you find him. You looked lost. Yes, I know, I'm a terrible, stupid person."

He had to be lying, though it was hard to square this whimpering hedge-fund manager with whoever had crushed Ilkka's head with a silver punch bowl. This guy was big, but he didn't look like he'd spent much time at the gym lately. Maybe it was the crank, but I couldn't get a fix on him. He was unshaven and wore a pinstriped suit jacket and trousers, creased button-down shirt, leather shoes stained white with road salt. It was a look incongruous with his feral amber eyes and the fact that he reeked of cheap vodka. He kept glancing at Gilda's unconscious form like it was the *Pietà* someone had taken a hammer to.

"Yeah, stupid just about covers it," I said at last. "Why were you at Baldur's place?"

"It's on my way home."

"To here? This your squat?"

He said nothing until the shovel poked him again. "Only for now. I lost my job, and then we lost our house. We have no family in Reykjavík, so we moved in here. The buildings are just going to waste. We haven't damaged anything."

"The girl's your daughter?"

"Élin. She's just a girl, please—"

"Anyone else here?"

"No. In some of the other places, maybe. People move in and out, squatting. I try to keep Élin away from them. It's difficult." He pushed a hank of blond hair from his face and looked at me beseechingly. "We've lost everything."

"Yeah? Ilkka and Suri and Bredahl lost more. Who killed them?"

The beseeching look hardened into an obdurate glare. I shifted, keeping a tight grip on the shovel. My skin was starting to itch from the crank. I raised my foot and pressed my boot's steel-capped toe against his groin.

"In the parking lot where Baldur died—you were holding something. What was it?"

He remained silent, then finally pointed at the table. I leaned over and saw an object behind the bottle of Pölstar, a wooden bowl with a lid, about six inches in diameter. Its lid was ornately carved with abstract swirls that, when I looked more closely, resolved into three interlocking, skeletal hands with a ghostly face in the negative space between them. I stuck the shovel under my arm and picked up the bowl.

"What is this?"

"An *askur*. An antique ash bowl. Very old. Five hundred years, maybe."

I ran my fingers across its carved top, over the whorls smoothed from god-knows-how-many other fingers over five centuries. The lid was hinged with silver and fastened by a tiny silver latch. I weighed it in my palm. "Is there something in it?"

"I don't know. I didn't open it."

I slid my fingernail beneath the silver hasp, then carefully raised the lid. Einar gagged and I covered my nose as a putrid stench filled the air.

The box contained a wad of red-and-white paisley cloth. I picked it up gingerly, saw that it wasn't paisley but the remnant of a white T-shirt, clotted with dried blood. I grimaced, then unfolded it.

Inside was a clenched human hand, its flesh the color of milky ice. The nails were painted indigo; there was a ring on the third finger, a thick silver band inset with a moonstone. Several blond hairs had snagged on the stone's setting. I raised the hand to the light and saw where the bone had been severed, frayed skin wrapped around tendrils of vein and tendon. She'd had delicate wrists; it wouldn't have taken much of a blade. Just a very sharp one. I bound the grisly relic in its soiled wrappings and replaced it in the wooden bowl, leaned on the shovel handle, and stared at Einar.

"Did you know whose that was?"

He shook his head without looking up.

"I do. Her name was Suri. She lived in Helsinki. I saw her there two days ago. She was murdered after I left. What is her hand doing in your antique bowl?"

"I don't know, I don't know." He lifted his head, his face stricken. "I didn't open it; I didn't know it was there."

"Did she?" I pointed at Gilda, still out cold.

"No! Of course not. I just arrived here; we hardly spoke. She wanted me to turn off the music and talk to her; we were arguing."

"About what?"

"About nothing! We were always arguing. About Élin; she was always worried."

"Did you hurt her?"

"What? No, of course not!" He stumbled to his feet, cheeks splotched with anger. He was younger than I'd thought, maybe thirty-five. With a better haircut and shave, he'd be someone you'd trust with your money, if you'd never seen the movie *Wall Street.* "Who the hell are you? Why are you here? Why did you follow me? Answer me!"

"I was with Baldur's sister. She's talking to the cops now. Either you tell me what happened, or I'll call them. Then you and Gilda will have something else to argue about."

His face went slack. After a moment he leaned back and gazed at the ceiling.

"It's my brother," he said. "Everything in the car—it's his. He's mentally ill. Schizotypal—it's a milder form of schizophrenia. He's supposed to take medication for it but he never does. He lives on his own in the highlands. I hadn't seen him in a while, almost a year. Then he called early this morning and asked if I'd pick him up at the airport. He wanted a ride to Kolaportið. He said he was going to meet some friends. It wasn't open yet but he said that was okay, so I got him at Keflavik and dropped him at the market and left. He said he'd call me later but he never did. I saw he'd left some things in the car but I didn't look at them; I was busy, I had some work to do downtown. Then when I was on my way home tonight I saw there had been an accident. I was curious, and . . ."

"Did he know Baldur?"

Einar ran a hand through his hair. "Of course. Everyone knew Baldur. Everyone here knows everyone. They did business together sometimes."

"Vinyl business?"

"*Nei.* Cocaine, mostly. Baldur knows people in Norway and Estonia, and my brother has trouble with drugs. He thinks they work better than his medication. Maybe they do, I don't know."

"Why would he kill Baldur?"

"How would I know?" Einar ran a hand through his hair and groaned. "God, this is horrible! Some drug thing?"

"What's your brother's name?"

"His given name is Jonas Broddursson. But since university, he calls himself Galdur."

Help Galdur.

The breath froze in my throat. "Galdur?"

"It's not his Christian name," Einar went on. "It's an old word that means magic, sorcery. But Jonas made it his name, declaring he is now a sorcerer. He went to university in Oslo to study astrophysics. Jonas is a kind of genius. But he got involved with the black metal scene there, and that was when he began to act strangely, maybe fifteen years ago. He was nineteen or twenty. I am a year younger, and I went to visit him once. He and his friends, they would all be at Helvete— you know, the store where all the famous black metal musicians would hang out. Before they were all dead." His mouth twisted slightly. "Back then, everyone wanted to believe in the Black Circle, black magic. Most just pretended to.

"But Jonas really did—he really thought it was true. He told me he had risen the Devil by sacrificing a man. He said he could kill people by looking at them. At first I thought he was just making it up, and then I thought maybe he was doing a lot of drugs. And he was. But really, it was the illness. They did a genetic study here; it showed that brilliant mathematicians are more likely to become schizophrenics. Our great-uncle, he went mad; he was a biochemist. In Jonas it was simply less severe. Or so it seemed."

"What about you?"

He bared his teeth in a humorless, vulpine grin. "I was also good at mathematics, but I went into the banking business. It would have been better for Jonas if he had done so as well. He went to prison in Norway for killing a man. He claimed it was self-defense, that the man had attacked him at a club. There were witnesses, people who tried to catch the man, but he ran away. He followed Jonas back to his flat and jumped him again, but this time Jonas beat him unconscious with a guitar. He broke his neck, then drained the blood from his throat and kept it in the refrigerator. That is where the police found it when they arrested him. Jonas said the blood was to raise the dead man, so he could use him as a sending—a ghost that would do his will."

"What kind of guitar was it?"

Einar scowled. "I don't know! An electric one. Obviously he was mad, so they hospitalized him, then sent him to a minimum-security prison on Bastøy Island. When he was released he returned here. He gets a disability from the government and lives in the interior, so he bothers no one. He is very antisocial. I was surprised when he called me from the airport."

I thought of the sixth photo, of Baldur's corpse, and the bodies in Ilkka's house. My stomach knotted. "Quinn—does your brother know him, too?"

"I'm sure he does. He has the stall with Baldur, yes? Jonas might have seen them both at Kolaportið."

"Would they have gone willingly with him?"

"Of course, yes—why not?" Einar raised his hands. "You have to believe that I had no idea about this or that Jonas would kill someone now, after all he's been through. I simply can't believe it."

"You just said he killed someone in Oslo!"

"That was manslaughter, not murder."

"When you picked him up at the airport—where'd he been?"

"Helsinki."

I swore furiously. "Is your brother rich?"

"Of course not. He lives on disability and a little money we inherited from our parents. But it's not expensive to fly to Helsinki. And he is permitted to travel. Within the Scandinavian countries you don't even need a passport if you're a citizen. You think he murdered Baldur for money?" Einar laughed. "He's not that crazy. Baldur has no money. No one here has money anymore."

So who was willing to pay half a million euros for Ilkka's photographs? For a minute we were both silent.

"Have you tried calling Quinn?" said Einar.

"I don't have a cell phone," I admitted. "Or his number. He said he'd come back for me this afternoon at Brynja's. He never showed up, and he never called there."

"He's your lover?"

"A long time ago, when we were in high school. We hadn't seen each other since then."

Einar shook his head. "My brother's friends, the only people he remained close to—they were from when he was young, in Oslo. Something ties us to the past."

He looked at Gilda, still out cold, then at me. His gaze fell upon my wrist, and he frowned. "Where did you get that?"

I raised my hand, the spiked band brazen in the dim light. "Brynja gave it to me; she has them in her store. Why? Do you have one?"

"No," he said slowly. "That was my brother's idea. His friends—his followers—they all wore them. It was a sign of loyalty, and that you had taken part in an initiation. There were only a few of them. And now Brynja has them in that elf shop?" He grimaced. "Everything is devalued, right? She's smart to sell them."

"She says no one buys them."

"Well, maybe that's good, too. Listen. I need to see Jonas. If he's in trouble, if he's really done this thing—Jonas will talk to me. You have to let me go to him."

"So call him."

"He has no phone either. He lives very primitively."

By now I was vibrating into methamphetamine overdrive.

"What if Quinn is with him, too? He and Baldur were both supposed to be at the market, but they never showed up. What if your brother kidnapped them and killed Baldur, but Quinn is still alive?"

"This is crazy." Einar's voice rose to a desperate pitch. "Quinn isn't with my brother! I have nothing to do with any of this. I want only to be sure that Jonas is okay."

"He is obviously not okay!" Einar stared at his hands, and I prodded him again with my boot. "I need to find Quinn. I'm going with you. You know where your brother is now?"

"You have no idea what you're doing! It's a long way from Reykjavík—five or six hours."

"I don't give a rat's ass how far it is."

"Oh, Jesus." He rubbed his eyes and pointed at the shovel. "Only if you promise not to hit me with that."

I looked at Gilda. "And she stays here."

Einar said nothing. I grabbed the bottle of vodka. We both stared at the carved wooden bowl on the table.

"Leave it," I said, and turned to go.

"No." Einar picked it up. "I don't want it here with Gilda or Élin. They know nothing of any of this. We can dump it somewhere in the country."

"Whatever. Let's go."

"Okay. But I need to get—"

I dug the shovel into his back. "You need to get in the fucking car."

He grabbed his overcoat. With a farewell glance at Gilda, he followed me outside.

20

The snow had diminished to freezing mist. Einar handed me the wooden bowl, hacked the driver's door free of ice, and retrieved the jumper cables.

"I hope I won't need them. But it's a long way if we have any car problems." He tossed the cables into the backseat, took the *askur*, put it into the storage area at the rear of the car, and covered it with the mat. "Phew! That stinks."

He slid into the driver's seat. I kept the shovel, braced to bash him if he looked at me cross-eyed, but Einar was too busy cursing to notice.

"Piece of shit. The defroster never works. And the wipers. And the heat."

He started to drive, sticking his head out the side window until the defroster thawed a fist-size spot on the glass. There wasn't much traffic, and no cops. I found myself compulsively counting headlights, something else crank is good for. When we got beyond the city limits, I counted streetlights, then houses, and finally lava formations. After a while I counted just formations that resembled human beings. A lot of these had extra heads or too many limbs or not enough. When it came to hallucinating, this country met you more than halfway.

Away from the city, the night sky cleared. The car's heat finally kicked in, and I relaxed somewhat. Einar wasn't much for small talk, which was fine by me. He stared fixedly out the window, his jaw set and expression grim.

"I should have called the police," he said once. "The *askur*—I should have taken it to them right away. If I did that . . ."

"Forget about it."

A glow appeared on the horizon—another city. Then the glow burgeoned into a silver dome and finally into a disk so brilliant it was like a hole punched in the sky: If you put your eye to it, you'd see through to a place that would blind you. I stared at it, amazed. "I've never seen a full moon like that."

"Yeah, it's beautiful," said Einar. "*Morsugur*—that's what they call it in old Icelandic. The moon that sucks the fat from your bones."

We drove for hours. I felt exhilarated, invincible, more intensely awake than I'd been in my entire life. In the moonlight I could see for miles, all the way to the ocean if I tried, though we were headed away from the coast, toward the highlands. All the bad shit that had come down since I left New York sloughed away. Anton, Ilkka, Suri, Baldur were just names in a newspaper, and who reads newspapers anymore? I pushed away the memory of what was in the carved bowl behind me, glimpsed Ilkka's white face in the moon, and looked past it to the mountains, leviathans breeching a silver sea. I shut my eyes and saw Ilkka's phantom novas blooming in the darkness, dead faces more beautiful than they ever had been in life.

It is easier for me to let them go, knowing that you have seen them.

I thought of Quinn, of how his presence had irradiated the

city for me thirty years before, imbuing it with a dark glamour that still clung long after Quinn had gone, long after the city itself had become a husk inhabited by the hip and the dead.

Now I gazed at an otherworldly landscape that Quinn had come to haunt as well, his scarred face gazing at me from the sky overhead and the scarified landscape below. Paved roads had long ago surrendered to gravel tracks that disappeared into a desert of snow-covered lava. Black spires like a forest of charred trees blotted out the stars near the horizon. I craved light, staring at the moon until my eyes ached, and finally sank into my seat with the shovel between my knees. I took a swig of vodka and held the bottle out to Einar. He shook his head.

"*Takk, nei.*"

I swallowed another mouthful. "So were you into black metal, too? That's what you were listening to back there, right?"

"Yeah, sure. Mostly I listened when I was young. Sometimes, like tonight, I like to hear it. I have to be in the mood."

"And that mood would be . . . ?"

"It's very cathartic. But black metal—its day has passed. The bands now are posers, just trying it on. Some bands I can still listen to. Enslaved. Emperor is always good. And Christ Beheaded. But that's all just nostalgia for when I was young."

I contemplated nostalgia for a band called Christ Beheaded. As someone who recalled the Exploding Mountbattens, I decided not to comment. I reached into my bag to grab one of the cassettes I'd nicked from Ilkka's place.

"Here, play this. It's . . . I dunno . . ." I tried to make out the handwriting in the moonlight. "Nuclear Holocausto. Do you know them?"

"Yeah, sure. Beherit, a Finnish band. He's their guitarist and singer."

He inserted the tape and cranked the volume. As a surge of feedback and growls shook the car, Einar pounded the dashboard with excitement.

"I saw them do this with the pigs' heads on the stage. It was amazing! Nuclear Holocausto drank blood!" He glanced at me. "Most women don't like this. Gilda, she hates it."

"It's okay." I cracked my window, hoping the din might disperse, like smoke. "Do you know a band called Viðar?"

"Of course. That's my brother's band."

I sat up, stunned. "You're kidding."

"No, it's true. They were never a real band; they never toured. They were the house band at a club in Oslo. Forsvar. Jonas and two of his friends who were over there for a while—they did that one album together. Then they split up. A guy named Hallmar, he still lives in Reykjavík. I forget the other guy. The owner gave them money to go into a studio." He frowned. "That album's very rare—only a few hundred copies. I don't even have one. Jonas played it for me when I visited him that first time; they'd just recorded it, and he was so excited. How did you hear of them?"

"I'm not your grandmother. I hear stuff." I punched the eject button and removed the cassette, found another, and squinted at the label. "This looks like it says Impaled Nazarene."

"Ah, they're great!" Einar grabbed the tape and shoved it into the player. "More Finns. The Finns are demented, you know."

I tried to pretend the noise pouring from the stereo was something more pleasant, like maybe a plane crash. Outside stretched an expanse of rock flensed of any vegetation, even moss or lichen.

Wind-carved snow formed waves beneath craggy overhangs; ice bridges spanned crevasses and slabs of stone smooth and sheer as though planed by infernal machinery. Frozen waterfalls cascaded from spars of rock the color of a scorched rose. For as far as I could see, in every direction, we were the only living things. Nothing moved except for eddies of snow and the black grit thrown up by the Land Rover's wheels. It was inconceivable to me that people would ever have chosen to set foot on a landscape that looked as though it had been tortured, set aflame, and burned till nothing remained but cinders and slivers of bone. The moon seemed a more likely habitation. I hadn't seen another car in hours. I turned to Einar.

"Where are we?"

"*Hvergi.* 'Nowhere.'" He tapped the wheel in time with the staccato drumming. "Hundreds of years ago a few homesteads were here beside the rivers. The ruins are still here. Outlaws lived here; you can read about them in the sagas. If you could survive in this wilderness for twenty years, you could return to your farm. Now hikers come in the summer, sometimes; it's only a few weeks, and there can be snow in August. But no one lives here except my brother."

A sign loomed out of the night, marking a gulley between ridges of snow on a rising plain between two vast plateaus, ghostly blue and lunar white.

OFæR! IMPASSABLE!

"That's if you don't have a four-by-four," said Einar as the Range Rover dove into the gulley. "We go everywhere."

"What are those mountains?"

"The big one's Langjökull." He pointed to the one on the left. "And that's Hofsjökull. They're glaciers."

"No shit. I never saw a glacier."

Wind-carved hollows in the snow revealed scabbed turf and funnels of ice. In the distance, plumes of white smoke streamed toward the horizon. The Range Rover slowed to a crawl and turned onto a plain where two frozen ruts stretched into the moonlit night. Once I thought I glimpsed a light shining within the white smoke, but it disappeared before I could determine if it was a house or vehicle or falling star.

"Are we close?"

"*Nei.* Not for a while."

I let both sides of Impaled Nazarene play out. I was afraid of silence, even more afraid that the radio would find nothing but static. When the cassette clicked back to side one, I ejected it and stuck in the remaining tape.

"This band's called Blot."

I hoped the monosyllabic name meant they'd represent Ilkka's progressive metal side—Can, Gong, Tool, Blot. Instead there was about a minute of hiss, followed by the indistinct drone of conversation, bottles clinking, heavy metal on the stereo—Metallica's "The Thing That Should Not Be." A party.

"Shit. Someone taped over it." I hit fast-forward. Metallica had now been turned off. I could hear the voices more clearly but couldn't understand them. A party. "What are they saying?"

Einar shook his head. "I don't know. Listen."

Men's voices. An argument. Shouting. A woman laughed. There was a cacophony of breaking glass, furniture being overturned, curses.

Then a man's voice rose above the others, angry at first, then wheedling, as though he argued with someone who refused to respond. His tone grew increasingly desperate and abruptly gave way to an anguished scream.

"What the hell is that?" I looked at Einar. He didn't return my gaze but stopped the Range Rover and sat listening while the engine idled. The taped screams became so frantic that I found myself clutching the door handle. "Jesus Christ, it sounds like they're killing him."

"Shut up."

Einar turned the volume as high as it would go. His face grew taut. I knotted my hands in my lap, straining to hear a second man's voice, guttural, reciting a monotonous refrain. Not chanting; more like he was talking in his sleep. As the screams grew fainter I heard a muffled cry and the sound of someone vomiting, then a raspy, panting breath that went on, unbearably, for several minutes.

Then silence.

My mouth was too dry to speak. I reached for the eject button, but Einar knocked my hand away. He snatched the tape from the deck, turned on the overhead light, and stared at the label.

"What was that?" I tried to grab the tape from him. "Blot— whose fucking band is that?"

"Shut up!" He jabbed the cassette at my face. "Where did you get this?"

"I found it—"

"Where?" He grabbed my hair. "Where did you find this?"

"Helsinki! Someone's house."

He stared at me, his pupils shrunken to pinpricks by the overhead light.

"You stupid cunt," he said, and slammed my head against the windshield.

21

I blinked, found myself slumped across the seat, my hands tied behind my back and my cheek sticky with blood. The window above me showed a dark wedge of sky smeared red and brown. As I pushed myself up, the passenger door opened in an icy rush and Einar dragged me into the snow, stopping when we were twenty feet away from the car before he let go.

"You can stand. Good." He was holding the shovel. "Now walk."

I kicked out, lost my balance, but couldn't catch myself: He'd bound my hands with a jumper cable. He grabbed my upper arm and pushed me in front of him. "Just walk."

I staggered a few steps while he remained where he was. When I paused to look back, he shook his head, grasping the shovel in both hands like a broadsword. "Keep going," he shouted.

I walked backward, slowly, so I could watch him, but he didn't move, just stood with the shovel in his hands and his loden-green overcoat flapping in the frigid wind. With every step, my boots punched through brittle snow, and something knocked against the back of my knees—the cable's metal grips. After I'd gone another thirty paces, Einar turned and walked to the Range Rover. Before he got inside he looked back at me.

"He's my brother."

His voice echoed across the plain as the Range Rover did a 180 and roared out of sight.

I looked for something to shelter behind but saw nothing save a small outcropping of barren rock. I lurched toward it, crouched in the leeward side, and tried to catch my breath. Cold won out over panic, just barely. I had to get my hands free, but my fingers were numb and wet, and the cable slipped through them whenever I tried to grab it. Pellets of sleet stung my face as the wind gusted, hard enough to knock me down. I jammed myself against the rock, my face inches from my knees, and fumbled with the cable until I finally managed to clamp one of the grips onto a finger.

I hardly felt it—not a good sign—but it made it possible to tug the cable through one knot and then another. Einar wasn't much of a Boy Scout. It seemed to take forever, but at last I shook the cable from my wrists. I unzipped my leather jacket and thrust my hands under my sweater, groaning: It felt like hot nails jabbing my skin.

Now I started to panic.

I wiped sleet from my eyes and stared at the snow-covered wilderness that stretched between two glaciers, the one to my left a whale breaching above an icy sea. The moon hung a hand's span above it—a setting moon, so that would be west. Straight ahead of me, through the lunar glitter of sleet and wind-driven snow, white smoke billowed steadily.

It was miles away, and seemed like far too much smoke for a wood fire, and where would you find wood to burn? And I couldn't imagine a power plant in this wilderness.

But then, until I came to Iceland, I would never have been able to imagine a place like this at all. I knew I had to keep moving. My wrist ached from the spiked bracelet Brynja had given me: The cold metal burned my skin. I struggled with numb fingers to unclasp it and stuffed it in my pocket, then pulled the collar of my sweater around my head to form a makeshift hood. I stretched the bottom of the sweater until it covered the top of my thighs, straightened, and stamped my feet.

My toes ached. At least I could still feel them. My face and hands were wet, my ass and legs freezing—one reason you don't see a lot of people attempting K-2 in skinny black jeans. Otherwise the layers of wool and leather had kept me dry, even if I was starting to shake with cold. I couldn't remember if shivering was supposed to be good or bad. All I knew about hypothermia was that you begin to feel warm and drowsy, then you lie down to sleep, and then you freeze to death. The rock wasn't enough to shelter me. There was snow everywhere, but it was too hard-packed to burrow into, and that would just be resigning myself to an ice coffin.

The only aspect of this disaster scenario I might have been able to rise above was the not-falling-asleep part. I huddled back against the rock and dug in my pocket for the crank, shoved my finger into the envelope, then jabbed as much as I could into one nostril after the other. It burned like acid, searing the back of my throat. I swallowed a mouthful of snow, something else I was pretty sure you weren't supposed to do. I wolfed down the chocolate bars I'd taken from Einar's car, tied the jumper cable around my waist, pulled my hands up into my sleeves, and staggered to my feet.

I started walking.

In toxic amounts, crank induces hyperthermia. I knew a guy who swallowed his stash to avoid being arrested, and when they got him into the ER, his core body temperature was 114 degrees Fahrenheit before it was lowered by ice blankets. I'd spent so much of my life wasted that I always assumed when it was time to check out, I'd be too fucked up to notice.

Now, the irony wasn't lost on me that I would be wide awake as I froze to death.

The wind was so powerful it was like forcing myself through an invisible wall. I was dimly aware of my head pounding where Einar had smashed it against the windshield, dimly aware of the blood frozen to a grainy crust on my cheek, and my wrists throbbing where they'd been chafed by the jumper cable.

But that was all background static to the wind. During World War II, the Nazis gave meth to soldiers, who'd fight until their legs were blown out from under them. Sometimes they wouldn't give up even then, dragging themselves along the ground with exposed bone and scorched flesh until their hearts gave out. I thought about that zombie army as I broke into a shambling run, head down, staring at the white ground in front of me and counting mindlessly to a thousand, losing track again and again. Fine snow and windblown sand streamed through the air like fog, but fog that bit my face like countless stinging insects. Every few steps I stumbled. Sometimes I fell. The moon had dipped below Langjökull, though the sky was still eerily bright. Reflected moonlight bounced from the snow-covered plain and made strange patterns in the air, like swooping birds. The screaming gale became indistinguishable from the sound of blood pulsing in my ears. I heard high-pitched cries— more birds, I thought; but of course there were no birds here.

Yet something hovered in the air a few yards in front of me, wings beating as it flung itself against the wind—the moon's black shadow, a raven.

I was starting to hallucinate. I rubbed icy grit from my eyes, not daring to halt. The bird was still there. I knew that seagulls would follow boats, hoping to score chum or other trash thrown overboard. Maybe this was an Icelandic vulture, waiting for me to die. I veered and stumbled over a lava mound. The raven followed, diving toward my face. I batted it away and it struck again, its talon piercing my cheek. I stopped, panting, turned and stumbled back the way I'd come as the bird continued to attack me. I covered my head with my hands and ran, dodging lava hummocks. The ground cracked beneath my boot, the skin of ice on a shallow stream, but I kept going until I finally collapsed, retching with fatigue.

When I looked up the bird was gone, and the moon. A few pale stars pricked a charcoal sky. The wind had died, and with it the snow. I couldn't feel my feet. I stamped them against the frozen ground until a prickle of sensation returned to my toes. I withdrew my hands from beneath my sweater, tried to straighten my clenched fingers, and kept walking.

In the distance smoke billowed, nearer than before, great clouds rolling across the horizon to fade into distant hills. A star shone through the smoke, brighter than the faint stars overhead. I wiped my eyes and saw that it was far too low upon the horizon to be a star. The highlands rose behind it, darker than the sky. To my left, the stream I'd forded widened into an ice-locked river, a serpentine channel that led toward the smoke. I followed this, the rocky ground giving way to knobs of lava encrusted with moss that glowed an improbable beryl green in the darkness. There were two long channels in the frozen turf—dry streambeds, I thought at first, but soon realized they were ruts left by vehicles.

I tried to run, but by now I could barely walk. My legs felt as though they'd been impaled upon steel spikes. A crust of rime formed across my sweater where my breath had frozen. My lungs and heart had fused into a solid burning mass lodged inside my chest. Spidery forms wriggled across my vision. I tripped and fell onto something smooth and circular—a tire. If it had been upright, it would have been nearly as tall as I was.

I looked up and saw an old Econoline van that had been converted to a 4 × 4, mounted on even bigger tires to loom above me like an antiquated space capsule. Beside it were several tarp-covered objects lashed with bungee cords, and what looked like the other part of the lunar landing pod—a snow-covered Quonset hut, its door surmounted by a sign covered with runic letters.

A column of light spilled from a window. I staggered toward the door and pounded as hard as I could until it swung open, and I fell to my knees in the snow.

22

A man shouted. I opened my eyes as someone tried to pull me to my feet.

"*Pétur! Getir tú hjálpa mér?*"

I kicked but my legs wouldn't move. I was in a room, dimly lit by a single kerosene lamp. After the endless dark outside I was blinded and saw only a blurred figure above me. A giant of a man, bearded, naked, and glaring.

"*Hver í veröldinni ert tú?*" I shook my head, and he demanded, "Who are you?"

My cracked lips couldn't form a reply. The man frowned, and his anger faded somewhat. "He's frozen! Pétur, help me get him into the bed."

A second man joined him, much younger—a boy, almost, twenty-one or -two. The first man hefted me in a fireman's carry and strode into another room.

It was dark there. The giant set me down on a bed. "You have hypothermia," he rumbled, his voice so deep it was as though the stones spoke. "You need to get out of your clothes so we can warm you."

I thrashed feebly as they peeled off my boots, socks, leather jacket. I heard a chink as something fell to the floor, and a low hiss from the big man. The boy, Pétur, pulled off my jeans and sweater and quickly stepped back.

"What the fuck? It's a woman!"

The older man stared at me. "Go heat some water for her to drink," he commanded. "Hot, not boiling. Put something sweet in it. Then get me some more blankets. And put the lamp on."

Pétur hurriedly lit another lantern and left the room. The big man slid into bed beside me.

"Don't be afraid. We have to warm you, but not too quickly or you'll die. Do you understand?" I groaned and tried to move away, but he pulled me to him, tugging the blankets over us. "Do you want to die? No? Then be still. I will not harm you."

The bed was still warm—someone had been sleeping there— and the man's body radiated heat like a stove. His broad chest enveloped mine, his long hair and beard scratched my face. He reeked of sweat and semen. "You're like ice," he said, and shouted for Pétur to hurry. "Just lie still."

As heat seeped back into my feet and hands I began to sob with pain. The big man reached down to cup my foot in one huge hand. "It hurts, yeah? That's good," he said. "That means the nerves may not be damaged. Try not to move...."

I drifted into a nightmarish state between wakefulness and delirium. My skin felt as though someone dragged a hundred soldering irons across it; my arms flailed uncontrollably. At some point I drifted into unconsciousness, then woke to the man running his hands across my body, as though checking a horse he might buy.

"You are warmer." He looked to where Pétur stood at the bedside, holding a steaming mug. "Let's see if you can drink this now."

He pulled me upright, cradling me against him like a child. He took the mug and sipped from it, nodded thanks at Pétur, and held it to my lips. "Here—"

Whatever was in it was black and sweet; hot, but not scalding. I gagged, but the man stroked my back and continued to bring the mug to my lips, until it was empty. He set it on the floor and took my face in his hands.

"Can you see me?" I nodded. "Can you talk? Do you know your name?"

"Yes. Cass." My throat felt as though I'd swallowed glass. "Cassandra Neary."

"Cassandra, okay, I'm going to let you sleep. I'll check back on you. We can talk later."

He withdrew and tucked the blankets lightly around me, lowered the lantern flame, and left. Pétur remained for a minute, staring at me in wonder.

"No one has ever walked here in the winter. Not even Galdur."

"Galdur?" I whispered, but the boy was gone.

Exhaustion won out over unease: I closed my eyes and tried to will myself to sleep. Instead I imagined myself with my feet rotted off and blackened stumps where my hands had been. When the man finally returned to check on me, I pushed myself onto a pillow.

"I need to get up."

He looked at me doubtfully. "Can you stand?"

"I think so. If you help me—"

"Wait—you need clothes to stay warm." He rummaged around the dim room, returning with a pair of jeans, a flannel shirt, a baggy Icelandic sweater, and heavy wool socks. "These are Pétur's;

they should fit."

I took the clothes then turned away, swearing when he tried to help me; I swore more loudly when I had to ask him to pull my arms through the sleeves and tug my socks on.

"This is so fucked." I shrugged into the sweater, trembling. "I can't even move my fingers."

"I think you'll be all right: You didn't get frostbite, which is incredible. The fact you are alive is incredible. Come in here; I'll get you more to drink."

I hobbled after him into the main room of the Quonset hut. It smelled of sulfur and wet wool, a compact space with two smaller rooms carved from it—the bedroom I'd just left and a bathroom. The curved ceiling was covered with rolls of insulation, and on to this were tacked pictures of stars and constellations, hundreds of them. Most had been printed from a computer, though there were several framed color photos, washed out by exposure to sunlight. It took me a minute to realize that the photos formed a star map, like what you see projected on a planetarium dome, showing all the constellations of the northern sky. There was a large telescope, too, in the kitchen area, and on the far side of the open room a set of amps, a drum kit, and an electric guitar.

But not a lot in the way of furniture. Bookshelves, some plastic storage bins. No TV. A pile of rocks in the center of the room, a makeshift hearth or cairn. Pétur was flopped in an armchair, staring at a laptop. There was a sofa and a desk with a flat-screen computer monitor. Sheepskin rugs on the floor. Another laptop vied for space on a table with dirty dishes, wineglasses, and an empty bottle, and there were cases of wine stacked beside the front door. A small gas cookstove. No refrigerator, but who needed one?

The entire back forty was a refrigerator. The only light came from kerosene lanterns that flooded the honeycombed walls in gold.

I pointed at the electric guitar. "You've gotta be off the grid here. How do you play that?"

Galdur regarded me coolly. At last he said, "There are solar panels on the roof. They are not very useful in the winter, so I run a generator a few hours a day when I need to. There's a hot spring not far away; I pipe water for heating and washing up. I do not have a lot of demands. If it wasn't for that"—he gestured at the guitar— "I could live without electricity. But some things I will not sacrifice."

He sank onto the sofa, ramrod straight. Sitting, he was nearly as tall as I was standing; broad shouldered, with arms as big as my calves and hands that looked as though they could crush a boulder like an acorn. He wore a black T-shirt and black jeans, heavy felted slippers. A bronze ring circled one upper arm. His brown hair was streaked with blond, his carefully trimmed beard gray flecked.

But he had an ascetic's face, saved from delicacy by a square chin and long, slightly slanted eyes of a shimmering topaz I'd only seen once before: the Marvel Comics version of his brother Einar. He made a fist and inclined his head in a salute. "I am Galdur. Who has sent you here?"

"Uh, no one." I grabbed a chair and sat. "I was . . . lost."

Pétur looked up from his laptop. "Lost? No one comes here, especially in winter."

"And no one comes here by mistake," said Galdur.

He stared at me fixedly. I tried to return his stare but gave up: In sixty seconds, I didn't see him blink. I looked at the photos on the ceiling, the Big Dipper so enlarged that each star seemed to have exploded into red fragments. I was thousands of miles from anyone who knew me, except for Quinn, who may well have been murdered by the same man who'd killed Baldur and the others; the same man who now, inexplicably, had saved my life. It was starting to hit me that maybe he hadn't done me a favor.

"I wandered off," I said slowly. "I'm a tourist, I didn't have a fucking clue where I was."

"Don't lie to me. Not even tourists are stupid enough to come to the highlands in winter on foot. You should be dead. No woman can survive, dressed like . . ."

He crossed the room, seized my leather jacket from a drying rack and shook it furiously, then kicked at my boots on the floor. ". . . like a cowboy. There are people lost here whose bodies are never found; did you know that? Icelandic trekkers who have climbed the Himalayas—in the winter *they* die here. So I ask you again—"

He flung aside my jacket and sat, regarding me with those vulpine eyes. "How did you come here? How did you come by this?" He held up the spiked bracelet. "Tell me!"

He threw the bracelet at me. I caught it, clutching it like a weapon. "Someone gave it to me. In Reykjavík."

"Who?"

"A woman in a tourist store. Brynja."

"Brynja?" Galdur looked taken aback. "Brynja Ingvarsdottir?"

"I don't know her last name. She owns a tourist shop. A friend of mine dropped me off there."

"The rune shop?" broke in Pétur. "The one at the edge of town?"

"I guess. She had a lot of stuff like that—books and rune

stones. Souvenirs."

"Is that who brought you here?" asked Pétur.

"Brynja would not leave the city if it was under nuclear attack," retorted Galdur. "And she doesn't know where I live; she doesn't want to know. So I ask you again: How did you come here?"

I flushed but said nothing.

"Did you follow someone? See anyone else?"

"Only a bird."

"A bird?" Galdur laughed. I glanced over to see Pétur watching me. He caught my eye and shook his head, almost imperceptibly.

"Yeah," I said. I was pissed that when I finally told the truth, no one believed me. "I saw a big black bird. A raven."

"You're lying." Galdur grabbed my sweater, pulling me until my face was inches from his. "No one sees a raven here in winter in the middle of the night."

"I did," I insisted. "I mean, maybe I was delirious, maybe I imagined I saw a fucking bird. But look—" I pointed at the gash on my face. "It clawed me—I tried to run and it attacked me."

Galdur let go of my sweater. He touched my cheek then drew closer to me, staring at the scar beside my eye. "What is that?"

"I was attacked a few weeks ago. It hasn't healed yet."

He stared at me pensively, then gestured at my abdomen. "You have a scar there, too; I noticed it when I was warming you. Show it to me."

I lifted the sweater and shirt, exposing the map of scar tissue and faded tattoo. Pétur stepped over to peer at it.

"'Too tough to die,'" he read. "That's no fucking lie."

Galdur shook his head. "Tell me your name again."

"Cassandra Neary—Cass."

"You're American?" I nodded, and Galdur turned away. "Cassandra was a seeress. Brynja, too. I don't know what this means."

Pétur stood. "It means I'm going to grab a smoke."

"Take her with you." Galdur got up and stalked toward the bedroom. "If she wants to run away, let her."

I felt like shit, but the confined space was making me feel claustrophobic. I hurriedly pulled on my leather jacket and boots and followed Pétur outside. He leaned against the Quonset hut, surrounded by cartons of empty wine bottles, and cupped his hands around a lighter.

"Smoke?"

"No thanks. Christ, my boots are still wet."

Pétur inhaled and narrowed his eyes, staring at the sky. Night had faded into the northern dawn, a sooty expanse of snow and rock broken by distant black crags and a bright ridge atop the highlands, shining like a blade where an errant ray of sun struck it. The wind blew scattered snowflakes and sent smoke streaming toward us across the plain.

"What's that smoke?"

"That's the hot springs." Pétur wore only an Icelandic sweater and jeans and Converse low-tops but seemed impervious to the cold. "It looks farther away than it is. Like the glacier looks closer than it is. In Iceland, everything is an illusion."

He laughed. Like half of Iceland's population, he could have been a model, clean-shaven with long, stringy black hair and azure eyes. I thought of the single mattress inside the hut. I wouldn't kick this kid out of bed, either.

"Do you live here?"

Pétur spat at the frozen ground. "Not in winter. It is possible, barely, to get here with a good truck, so I visit. I'm at university in Reykjavík, but we're on Christmas vacation now. By the old calendar, this is midwinter night, Jöl, and Galdur wanted me to be here. I come every month or so to make sure he's still alive, also to play music. He's one of the greatest guitarists in the world, you know that, right?"

"Sure."

"That's why he gets so angry: Sometimes people try to find him, you know? Like a pilgrimage. But that's in the summer. I'm here then, so I send them away. 'What, you're looking for Galdur? You must be crazy! No one could live in this place. Go back and look in Reykjavík. Or Oslo.'"

He laughed again, then cocked his head. "But yeah, you know, it's bad fucked that you're here. He really doesn't like it. A few years ago a guy showed up, he wrote for *Terrorizer* magazine? Galdur beat him so bad he had to be taken out by rescue helicopter."

"Jesus. Did he go to jail?"

"No, he said it was self-defense. Because the guy came inside to wait while no one was here, and when Galdur came home he found him in the living room. With, you know, a camera and digital recorder—very dangerous weapons! He was unconscious when they took him out. Don't feel too bad; he wrote a good story out of it, even though Galdur destroyed his equipment." Pétur tossed his cigarette, a spark against the gray sky. "He had trouble with the law before, in Norway, but here in Iceland, I think they would rather not have to be responsible for him."

"Yeah, I heard about that shit in Oslo." I hesitated. "Do you know a guy named Quinn? American, about my age?"

Pétur shook his head. "No, sorry."

"He has a table at the flea market; he sells old records."

"Oh, yeah." Pétur brightened. "Yeah, sure—he works with the albino, right?"

"Yeah, that's him. Does he ever come out here?"

"No. I tell you, no one comes here. And Galdur, mostly he stays away from all the old music scene. He goes into Reykjavík a few times a year, to get supplies. He records music here—mostly ambient stuff he does on his laptop. We met at the upstairs room at Sirkus a few years ago. A great bar, but they closed it." He grimaced and spat again. "Fucking bastards. I went there a lot. I heard Galdur sometimes went, too, because no one bothered him, especially after that *Terrorizer* guy got pounded. I could not believe it when I was there one night, and I looked over, and he was drinking a glass of wine. I had a few beers so I wasn't afraid. My friends thought I was crazy, but I went over and talked to him for a long time. That was how we met. The thing no one understands about Galdur— he wants them to believe he is, you know, the man of stone and ice. Nothing touches him, he is above the world, he is god of all he can see. It's that mathematician brain: Everything can be explained by cold logic. Maybe some things, but not everything. Not me."

He grinned, and I huddled into my jacket, shivering. "If he's so logical, why'd he flip out about the raven?"

"That's what I mean. Probably it was because of the Odin thing. Ravens are sacred to Odin, and Galdur's very spiritual; he is a follower of Ásatrú. Then he sees your eye, and of course Odin has only one eye. At first we think you are a man, but you are a woman, and Odin too dressed as a woman and practiced women's magic.

"So when you show up at the door in the middle of the night and say that a raven brought you—well, Galdur will be very agitated. You know what else is weird? I only got here yesterday, too. I might have seen you hitchhiking, right?" He laughed. "A real traffic jam at Lindvidi."

"What's that?"

"The name of Galdur's house. It means 'wide land.' In the sagas, Lindvidi is where Viðar lives—he is the god of silence and vengeance—so of course it's where Galdur lives." He turned to kick at the Quonset hut's wall. "He brought this out from the Keflavik airbase a long time ago, before it closed. It's sweet, huh?"

"Yeah. Silence and revenge, huh? I just thought it was a good name for a band."

"It's a great name. Viðar is more famous now than when Galdur started it. The only band Ihsahn said was as good as Emperor. Some people say better. That guy from *Terrorizer*, when he wrote his story he said that the greatest true Norwegian black metal artist is not Norwegian, but Icelandic."

"I like their stuff." I looked past him, to the wall of steam erupting from the horizon. "That song on their first album, where you can hear voices in the background."

"That would be their only album. That's the song most people know, but there's some bootlegged stuff; it's fucking great. They must have kicked ass live. I wish I could have seen them, but I was, like, five. But that song—every time I talked to Galdur about it, he just says Blot is holy and we don't talk of these things."

" 'Bloat'?"

"*Blot* means 'sacrifice.' An old Norse word. In Ásatrú, it means the midwinter feast and ritual. Once upon a time, something else."

But definitely not a prog-rock band.

"I have to get something out of my car," Pétur announced. He headed toward the back of the Quonset hut. I caught up with him as he opened the door of a badly dented SUV and pulled out a large cooler. "I bring my own supplies. Galdur can live on wine and salted fish, but not me. Grab that six-pack, will you?"

He set the cooler down in the snow outside the front door, retrieved a plastic quart container and a paper bag, and took the six-pack from me. "I'm ready for breakfast. Are you doing okay?"

I shrugged. "I could be worse."

He looked at the raw landscape around us, the snow glowing blue and gold as the sun edged above the horizon, and turned back to me. "How the hell *did* you get here?"

"Good drugs," I said as we went back in.

I was relieved to see no sign of Galdur inside. The bedroom door remained shut. I drew a chair up to the table while Pétur made coffee and put out bowls and plates.

"Skyr." He set the plastic container in front of me. "Icelandic yogurt."

It tasted more like sour cream, but I wasn't going to argue. He'd brought some pastries, too, and bread and cheese and some kind of salami. It was the best food I'd had since leaving New York. Almost the only food. The coffee was decent, too.

"What day is this?" I asked.

"Monday. Why?" Pétur laughed. "You have to be somewhere? Good luck."

"No. It's just hard to tell; it's always so dark. And these windows don't help." I pointed at the small panes near the front door, all choked with snow.

"Yeah. I tell him, you'd get more light in an igloo. He doesn't care. There's never anyone else here to complain, except me."

"Doesn't his brother ever come?"

"What, Einar? He's not welcome here. Galdur hates him. Everyone hates him. Einar came visiting in October, right after the crash. He needed money and he had a crazy idea that Galdur would help him. He wanted Galdur to release the Viðar album with some new tracks. When Galdur said no, Einar argued with him about doing a concert—you know, a special gig at the Iceland Airwaves festival. They would make a lot of money, and Einar would record the live show and release it on DVD, then he'd make even more money. I thought Galdur would kill him."

"You were here?"

"No. But from the way Galdur talked about it afterward . . . he went berserk. So I would not mention Einar's name to him. I wouldn't mention Einar to anyone. He's one of the motherfuckers who screwed this whole country." Pétur's face grew red. "He and Galdur, they fell out a long time ago. I don't know what happened. But if you know Einar, you'll have a good idea: He's a fucking arrogant asshole. He's one of the útrás. What we call 'outvasion' Vikings, the bankers who stole everyone's money and used it to buy English football teams and Porsches and build themselves mansions. Everyone in Iceland hates them. You can tell their houses because people throw red paint on the walls. Four years ago we were one of the richest countries in the world. Now it's horrible: We have lost everything. My mother took investment advice from Einar, and she lost her home. Not Galdur—Galdur wouldn't give him one krónur. But some people trusted Einar because, you know, he is a fucking banker and he studied in America."

He laughed bitterly. "They fucked us, and now we are supposed to pay off their gambling debts? Do you know what it would cost to do that? Fifty thousand dollars for every person in Iceland. Einar had a house in Greece, a big new mansion here. His wife went to New York for a boob job, and so did his daughter. Now the house is repossessed, and the place in Greece—who knows? And he owes money to some people in the Russian mafia. So no, Einar is not welcome here."

He gathered the plates and stacked them in a plastic tub. I finished my coffee and tried to square Pétur's account of Einar with Quinn's, and both of those with the aging black metal fan in a Dolce&Gabbana suit, squatting with his wife and daughter in an abandoned construction site. The hardest part was imagining Galdur and Einar as brothers. The two looked alike, but the resemblance seemed to end there, except for their gift with numbers and the ability to scale down their domestic needs to kerosene and alcohol.

Also, the inexplicable fact that they shared a love for tremolo guitar and blast-beat drumming. Maybe there was something in Reykjavík's sulfurous water supply that contributed to seasonal affective disorder on a mass scale, but the predisposition toward musical anhedonia still didn't seem to have caught on here the way it had back in Norway.

It all made me miss the sunny optimism of The Smiths.

I stood and paced the room warily, trying not to make any noise that might disturb Galdur. I thought of Quinn, and for the first time in decades, maybe, felt on the verge of tears. I should have forced him to take me with him Sunday morning. I wouldn't be trapped here, in the middle of an ice desert. Or I'd have talked him out of meeting Baldur; we'd have found a bar and gotten shit-faced and fallen back into bed, or boarded a plane for someplace warm. Baldur would be dead, but we'd be gone to ground in Greece or Turkey or the Costa del Sol. We'd throw the dice and begin again.

I knew that all of these scenarios were impossible. Quinn was wrong: I could see into the future, but all I ever saw was my own dead gaze staring back. I glanced at Pétur, sweet-faced, spooning Skyr from the container as he leaned against the sink. It was difficult to think of him shacking up with a serial killer; almost as tough to imagine as him shacking up with a legendarily brutal musician who'd beaten a man to death with a guitar.

The Quonset hut had only one door: If I fled, I'd die in the wilderness. My only hope would be to steal the key to one of the vehicles—Pétur's, preferably—let the air out of the Econoline's tires, and hightail it across the desert. It was a stupid idea, but less stupid than dying. I looked for something that might be Pétur's—a coat or backpack—someplace he might stow a spare key. I saw nothing except for my own jacket slung across the sofa. I'd wait till Pétur stepped out for another cigarette, then do a more thorough search.

I distracted myself by perusing Galdur's books, which were impressive for a rock musician. He had hundreds of volumes, in English and Icelandic—abstruse works on applied mathematics, astronomy, navigation; archaeological monographs; tomes on excavations of Viking sites in Norway and Great Britain; Icelandic folklore and the sagas. Unlike Brynja's New Age bunk, these were nearly all from university presses, or scholarly texts published in the nineteenth and early twentieth centuries.

I pulled out a book on human sacrifice in northern Europe. The dust-jacket photo reminded me of the one in Ilkka's living room. A bog burial, different photo, same body, with its flaxen hair and broken spear in the crook of one leathery arm. The Windeby Boy. There were more photos inside: bog bodies with mutilated faces and decapitated heads; skeletons sitting cross-legged, minus their skulls; skulls that had been impaled on metal pikes then buried. Their gaping lower jaws made them appear to be screaming.

But the faces on the bog bodies seemed weirdly peaceful, even those who still bore nooses around their necks or whose throats had been severed to expose blackened vertebrae. They reminded me of Ilkka's Jólasveinar photographs; their subjects human, but their deaths so far beyond imagining that the images possessed the abstract purity of a funerary stela or ancient paleoglyph.

I replaced the book and stepped over to the indoor cairn. It didn't seem any more out of place than the electric guitars or drum kit in this weird little world. A carved wooden disk sat atop rocks chosen for their symmetry: black lava, bluish granite, round stones that looked like oversize, freckled eggs. The wooden disk reminded me of the antique *askur* with its gruesome souvenir: It had the same motif of the gripping beast. A few artifacts were carefully arranged on it, along with a cell phone. An iron blade, dimpled with rust, its edge gnawed by the centuries; a bronze band that looked as though it had broken off from something bigger, like a sword or helmet. I picked up another object, too small to be a weapon, the width of my hand and also made of iron, with a pair of tiny tongs at one end and a narrow blade at the other—an ancient surgical tool, maybe, like a scalpel. Heavy for its size, it would have demanded a steady grip and steadier eye.

"That's mine, sorry." Pétur crouched beside me, picked up

the cell phone, and flipped it open. "That's the only place I never lose it. You asked what day it is, and I thought I better check. Yes, it's Monday. It doesn't work here; some places in the highlands you can get reception, but not here." He lowered his voice to a conspiratorial whisper. "I think Galdur blocks it with his mighty brain."

He laughed, set the phone back on the cairn, and walked off. I replaced the scalpel beside it, then saw something protruding from between the stones—a small white knob, like an ivory tuning key. It was wedged in tight, so I tugged until it slithered free, then dropped it, startled, catching it before it could hit the floor.

It was a skeletal hand, the slender finger bones mottled like tortoiseshell, five cold spindles. Unlike Suri, whomever this belonged to had died long ago. I placed it beside the ancient scalpel and noticed a slab of crystal beside the cairn, the size and shape of a piece of old-fashioned block ice, with a hardcover book on top of it. The book was open, its pages displaying Icelandic text that faced an English translation.

> . . . blood from a man whose death was not mourned and inscribe first upon one's own right hand and then upon the tombstone these staves in blood. You must do this on the fourth day of the fourth week of summer, when the earth is yet fresh. The dead man will awaken, and you must take care the earth thrown up by his awakening does not touch your feet, else you will walk the same path he does. You must ask him, Who mourns you? And if he names a man or woman or child, you must cast the staves upon him and depart. But if he is silent, you must observe when the corpse-

froth begins to spill from his mouth and nostrils, being
certain to lick it from them before he . . .

"That does not work." I cringed at the rumble of Galdur's
voice, but he only took the book from my hand and set it aside.
"This, however, does."

He picked up the block of crystal. It had been roughly polished,
and I could see striations within it, like threads spun from the
rock. "This is a sunstone. Iceland spar—they mine it in the east. In
ancient days the Vikings used it to navigate. It is a naturally polar-
izing lens; you hold it to the sky when clouds hide the sun, and it
changes color, so you can determine the sun's location. Come, I'll
show you."

We walked outside. Pétur was behind the building, bent over
something that looked like a lawn mower. The sun had been swallowed by clouds the color of the lava fields near Keflavik. It was
difficult to tell where the sky ended and mountains began.

Galdur looked at me. "Which way is north?"

I shrugged. "Damned if I know."

He held the crystal in front of his face as though it were a pair
of binoculars, scanned the sky, and handed the stone to me.
"There—see?"

I looked through the crystal and saw a brilliant, cyanic flare in
its heart. "That's amazing." The radiance faded as I turned in the
opposite direction. "Does it work at night?"

"Only to confuse you, if you were trying to navigate by the
stars. Look at Pétur there."

I did. "Holy shit—it doubles everything."

"It's called birefringence. Double refraction. The crystal splits the light in two, and each beam travels at a different speed. So even though they look the same, they are different. One is an ordinary ray. The other is an extraordinary ray."

"That's fucking amazing." I turned the crystal on Galdur and saw his face doubled. "Can anyone tell the difference between the two rays?"

"No." He took the crystal from me. "'Anyone' cannot. But I can. For years no one believed our ancestors could have used these to steer by. Then, very recently, scientists proved that what I have always known is true. When the power grid fails, and all of those satellites have fallen from the sky, I will still be able to find true north."

He smiled, but I couldn't tell if he was joking. A roar split the silence and I jumped.

"The generator," Galdur shouted as Pétur walked toward us. "Go in and take a shower while you can."

I did, in scalding water, and kept a close eye on the stall door, then dressed in my own clothes, now dry. I still didn't know if Galdur's sudden conversational flashes were meant to be reassuring or if he was just biding his time to work me over with an Iron Age scalpel. I thought of my camera, in Einar's Range Rover or tossed somewhere in the ice desert, along with my passport and Ilkka's photos, all save the one picture hidden in my jacket lining. I stuck my hand into my pocket, but there was no envelope of crank there, no Focalin or anything else that might tweak my brain chemistry enough that I could keep myself from imagining all the ways I could die. I pulled on my boots, ran my finger across one steel-tipped toe, and returned to the main room.

With the generator on, several electric lights had blazed to

life. Galdur had set the sunstone back upon the altar, upright so
that it resembled a piece of contemporary sculpture. I heard the
anodyne hum of an amp. Galdur stood tuning his guitar as Pétur
settled behind the drum kit and threw out some one-handed rolls.
I crossed my arms and watched, nodding as Pétur grinned.

"You're good," I said.

"Yeah, I know." He shook his hair from his face, and they began to play.

Pétur was great. And he was fast, his sticks ricocheting between
skins and snare in a blur.

But Galdur was incredible. He had that trademark black metal
sound down cold—tremolo picking, when you pluck the same
string repeatedly to produce a single note. You hear the same effect in
traditional Irish music, where it's usually done on a mandolin. But
the most famous exemplar is probably Dick Dale's work on "Misirlou," which he first did live, on a bet that he couldn't play an entire
song using only one string. You might think it's a long way from the
King of the Surf Guitar to Norwegian black metal, but music
makes these cosmic leaps all the time. "Misirlou" originated in
Smyrna: Dick Dale had seen his Lebanese uncle play it using only a
single string on an oud. Every electric guitar chord roaring down
the last fifty years, from Hendrix to Buckethead, is an echo of that
tremolo, and I'd kick the chair out from under anyone who claims
there's a better guitarist than Dick Dale.

Galdur came pretty fucking close. From the wrist up, his arm
was completely motionless; only his fingers moved, digits on a disembodied hand. I moved close enough to get a better look at his ax,
an original 1957 Strat, maple neck, alder body with that two-tone
sunburst finish. A guitar worth fifty grand; an original pickguard

for one will cost you four thousand bucks on eBay, if you're lucky. This one still had all its white Bakelite pickup covers and knobs; the vinyl ones they started using as replacements turned yellow after a few years. Galdur was shredding it in a homemade Quonset hut with an amp powered by a gas generator, for an audience of one, backed up by a kid who looked like he'd been air-dropped in from an Icelandic Gap advertisement.

It was maybe the greatest musical experience of my life. Tremolo done right can sound like two guitars, not one: When I closed my eyes, I could imagine an entire band filling the room in front of me. After a few minutes, Galdur let the last few notes drain off into reverb. He adjusted the amp; Pétur dropped his sticks and started to drum with his fingertips, now and then tapping the edge of the cymbal so it rang softly, like a distant bell echoing through steady rain. I could hear the generator's muted drone above a sudden rush of wind and feel the Quonset hut tremble slightly, as though it, too, were a bell that had been struck.

After a minute Galdur joined in with a single plucked note and then a repeated minor chord. He'd turned the volume low, so it took a while for me to recognize the same insinuating strains I'd heard first on Quinn's turntable and then in Einar's Range Rover. He played with his head bent over the guitar neck, tawny hair obscuring his face. Pétur nodded and after some time picked up his sticks again. The guitar chords thundered into a crackle of feedback as Galdur edged back to nudge the volume knob with his foot.

He began to sing, a resonant baritone that bore no trace of the choked snarls I'd heard on the albums at Quinn's stall. I couldn't understand the Icelandic words, but he sang in such a low voice I could hardly hear him anyway. Pétur mouthed the words along with him, eyes squeezed shut. Without warning, the electric lights went out, and the amp. Outside, the generator fell silent.

Pétur looked at Galdur. The only sign that Galdur had noticed was that he stepped closer to the drum kit, and Pétur quickly picked up the beat again. Instead of growing softer, the unamplified Strat actually sounded louder: I could feel that maple slab board resonating in my bones. Before, the kerosene lamps seemed to give everything a bright, varnished gloss. Now their glow seemed dulled, as though the glass chimneys were choked with ash. Pétur's shadow flowed into that of the drum kit, looming against the wall behind him, like the mountains etched against the winter sky.

Galdur's shadow leapt like a flame, only to disappear when he lifted his head, eyes closed, and cried out a string of words—a list of names. He looked anguished, as though he struggled to tear something from the Strat's neck, and the guitar fought back.

I've seen a million guitarists work this angle onstage, and they always look like idiots. Galdur looked terrifying. If someone distracted him from whatever internal battle he fought with the music, he'd lunge for the interloper's throat. I froze, afraid to draw attention to myself. The music rose and fell, Galdur's guitar quickening with the howling wind outside. The sound grew monotonous, hypnotic; more than once my eyes began to close.

To distract myself, I stared at the ceiling, first at the photographs that comprised Ursa Major, and then at the only other constellation I recognized, Orion. Small photos of the stars represented his flexed bow and raised sword; a separate photograph of three stars formed Orion's belt. These stars were much brighter than the rest and also much larger.

It took a moment to realize they weren't stars that made up this constellation, but faces. Galdur, much younger but still glowering, his pale eyes an uncanny, bleached white. Ilkka, his dark hair long and straight, eyes invisible behind glasses splintered silver from a camera's flash. The third face didn't belong to a living man at all. It was a skull, cupped in their upraised hands like a trophy. Tufts of black hair protruded from desiccated skin, and a string of tendon stretched between its jaws. Something that resembled a rind of dried fruit clung to one side, with a bright spar dangling from it—a silver earring.

A wall of black water hit me, the ozone stench of damage. My ears rang, a chime that bled into the tremolo flutter of a guitar. Galdur raised his head, hair swept back from a face streaked with sweat. His topaz eyes flared, his mouth moved, but I couldn't hear what he was saying. A note welled inside me as though I had become a sounding board. The kerosene lamp behind him swayed, and I saw that its base was not rusted metal but the pitted globe of a skull, liver colored and banded with leather. The drums fell silent.

"Now, that's what they call an evil chord." Pétur stared at me, head cocked. "You okay?" He turned to Galdur. "She looks sick."

Galdur slapped the Strat's neck. A guitar string snapped as the chord flattened into a metallic *thunk*. Frowning, he glanced at me, then crouched over the instrument, removing a string winder from the guitar case. After a minute he stood, wound the broken string into a shining coil, and slipped it into his jeans pocket. He set the guitar against the wall, switched off the powerless amp, and stepped toward me.

"What did you see?" he asked.

I shook my head, and he grabbed my chin. "You saw something—don't lie to me."

I twisted to point at the ceiling. Galdur looked up, then back at me, his face torn between rage and fear.

"How do you know this?" He grabbed my arm. "How do you know *Seiðhr*, our ways?"

"Don't you fucking touch me," I shouted, and pulled away.

For a moment I thought he'd strike me. Instead he turned and strode across the room. The bedroom door slammed. I walked shakily to where the guitar leaned beneath the skull lantern and stared at the lamp's lunar-white flame, a pulsing blue heart. Pétur came up behind me.

"What does that mean?" I asked without looking at him. "'Saythe'—what he called me."

"*Seiðhr*. It is what I spoke of before—sorcery." He touched the lantern's base. "I mean, if you believe in it."

"You don't."

I turned to him, and he shrugged. "I believe that he believes in it. He didn't make it up: You read about it in the sagas. *Seiðhr* means 'sorcery.' But it is, hmm, more like seeing things, you know?"

"Like clairvoyance?"

"Yes, I think so. It is like a kind of seeing, or a kind of singing, that makes the forms of things unseen visible. It is usually women's magic, but sometimes powerful men practice it too. Like Galdur."

"So you're another one majoring in paganism?"

"God, no. I'm studying business and Chinese. But we talk about it a lot. Well, Galdur talks, and I listen. Mostly I just want to play the drums. Some of it makes me uncomfortable. It's misogynistic, a bit. And other things. In black metal, a lot of the people are homophobes." I snorted. "Yes, I know. Galdur is a complicated person."

"No shit."

"He's changed a lot." Pétur sighed. "People who knew him back then—in Oslo—the things they've told me, I can't believe."

"Like almost beating a rock journalist to death?"

"That guy should have known better." Pétur's blue eyes glittered. "He should not have come here."

"Yeah, sure. Guy was just asking for it, right?"

My irony didn't translate: Pétur nodded in agreement. "Sure. But that was a long time ago. Galdur spends all his time now studying or looking at his telescope."

I ran a finger across the skull's rounded base. "I assume this is real—someone you know?"

"It's from Gotland, Sweden. It's very ancient. From a burial."

"Very tasteful. I can see a whole line of these at Barneys."

"He collects things like that. Viking artifacts. He showed you the sunstone." Pétur shook his head. "I'm surprised, you know? That he's speaking to you at all."

"I'm surprised he didn't deck me. And you know, he's not speaking much at the moment." I checked to make sure the bedroom door was still closed. "Listen—I've really, really got to get to the city. I have to catch my flight back to New York. Can you give me a lift or something? I'll pay you." I patted my empty pocket and tried to look ingratiating, then pointed at his drum kit. "You can tell me how you got into this whole death metal trip."

"Black metal." Pétur frowned. "Look, I can't leave. I told you, I just got here. It's my only free time: I have to return to classes at the end of the week."

"This is totally fucked." I kicked the wall in frustration. "I can't be here. This is all a mistake."

"But you are here. Maybe it's your *wyrd*." He tapped the skull lantern. "Everything you've ever done, coming back to bite you in the ass. That's what Galdur would tell you, anyway."

"Yeah, well, that would be just about my goddamn luck."

I paced back to the center of the room. I felt exhausted and suddenly ravenous. But I couldn't see much that looked like food, not unless you counted those cases of wine beside the door. Iron-gray light seeped through the windows, canceling out the glow of the kerosene lamps. Even indoors, I was trapped in this infernal, endless dusk. I looked up and scanned Galdur's handmade star map. There were other black-and-white images there, stapled alongside the printouts of constellations unknown to me.

And while I couldn't see them clearly, I discerned faces in the photographs, a telltale burst of radiance sparking from an eye or tooth. I walked to where Pétur had settled on the sofa with his laptop and nudged him.

"Who are those pictures of?"

He glanced up. "I don't know. Friends of Galdur's, I guess. I never really looked at them."

The bedroom door opened. We both looked over to see Galdur pulling on a black anorak. He gave Pétur a sharp look.

"I'm going to put more gas in the generator. You obviously didn't check when you turned it on."

"I did, it was almost empty. The gas can was empty too."

"There should be some in the van. You should have checked first." Galdur pulled up his hood and walked outside.

I turned to Pétur. "He's going to siphon gas from the van?"

"No—he stores extra containers in it so they don't get buried by the snow. I don't think there's any left; he hasn't been to Reykjavík for a long time. Or anywhere else," he added.

"I thought he just got back from Helsinki."

"Helsinki?" Pétur laughed. "I don't think so! He's never been to Finland, I don't think. And he hasn't been to Norway in years. When he was young he did time on that island prison, Bastøy. Manslaughter. I suppose he could return to Oslo if he wants, but he always tells me how much he hated it there and would never go back. Sometimes a promoter will try to get in touch with him, to see if he will perform, but he always says no. And of course he lost his passport. I wanted him to come with me to Rome for the holiday, and he couldn't find it. But he never travels, so it's not a problem."

"He never travels? Are you sure?"

"Yes, of course. He wouldn't go now, anyway. Jöl night, and he knew I was coming this week. No, he would never go to Helsinki," he ended with certainty. "He has bad memories about someone there."

I stared at the floor, cracked laminate made to look like wood. It had started to peel in yellowing strips that resembled fingernail parings. Frigid wind blasted into the room as the front door opened and Galdur stormed in, his hair and anorak covered with snow.

"What is this?"

To my shocked amazement, he held up Ilkka's Speed Graphic camera. I had a glimpse of my own face in its reflector before he set it down, then threw something at me—the *askur*—followed by my satchel. The *askur*'s lid flew off, its grotesque relic spilling onto the floor. Pétur gagged and pulled his T-shirt over his face. I fell to my knees and grabbed my satchel, pulled my camera from the nest of wadded clothing and checked that it was intact, then clambered to my feet.

"Where did you find this?" I demanded.

"It is yours?" Galdur's cheeks had gone pale with fury. "I found it where you put it—in the van." He picked up the hand, walked to the door, and tossed it out into the storm. "Along with that. And my *askur*, which was stolen from me last fall."

"The van? What the hell are you talking about? I've been inside this whole time. It was—"

Too late I tried to snatch my bag. Galdur grabbed it, turned it upside down so that my clothes went flying, along with the bulky cylinder wrapped in my shirt. He swooped on this, ripping the T-shirt open so that Ilkka's prints scattered across the floor. Pétur caught one and stared at it, dumbfounded. Galdur bent to pick up another just as I reached for it. He straightened, lunging for me.

"What is this? What have you done? Why do you have these things?"

"Einar," I gasped.

He dragged me to the wall, pinning me there. "Einar? My brother Einar? What are you saying?"

"Your brother kidnapped me." I fought to keep my voice steady. "In Reykjavík. He said he was coming here and then he dumped me out there somewhere—" I gestured at the door. "He left me to die. I walked here; I don't know how but I did. That's all I know."

"No." Galdur shook his head. "This is your bag, your cameras. These clothes are yours, yes? And these photos—how did you get these photos? Tell me."

So I told him. At the news of Ilkka's death he grabbed me

again. I thought he'd strangle me, but Pétur pulled him away. Finally I fell silent. Galdur remained where he was, breathing heavily. Then he slapped me, hard enough that blood sprayed from my nose across the wall.

"Again. I want to hear it again."

I tried to stanch the bleeding with my sleeve and recounted it all a second time. Pétur retreated to the couch but said nothing. His gaze flicked from me to Galdur and then to the photo in his hand. By the time I was done, Galdur's tawny eyes had grown so bloodshot they appeared crimson in the lantern flame.

"You're lying," he said.

"Lying? Who the hell could make this shit up?"

Galdur didn't reply. He stepped away, staring up at the trompe l'oeil constellation formed by the photograph of him and Ilkka and their trophy skull. His face contorted—with rage, I thought, and I flinched, fearing another blow. But when he turned to me once more, I saw that he was weeping.

"This should not have happened," he whispered.

"What in hell *did* happen?" Pétur shook his head, holding up the Jólasveinar photo of the man beneath the ice. "Who is this man? Who killed him?"

"I don't know who he was. A vagrant," said Galdur. "We found him in the forest one day, where he should not have been. Near my friend's cabin. He was drunk and propositioned me."

Pétur gave a sharp, disbelieving laugh. "And you killed him?"

Galdur turned that malefic, unblinking gaze on Pétur. I edged away, but Galdur didn't seem to notice. Neither did Pétur, who returned Galdur's stare fearlessly.

"Yes," said Galdur. "I do not regret it. I made an offering: His death was a gift. The salmon were very grateful."

"I can't believe this." Pétur began to pace, running his hands through his long hair. "Do the police know?"

"No one knows," said Galdur.

"Was Ilkka there with you?" I asked. "In the woods?"

"Yes, of course. Ilkka was always there. It was two, three months in the winter; we moved from one place to another place. There are always people who are where they should not be."

"Why did you stop?"

Galdur's gaze remained fixed on Pétur. "The police began paying attention to other people we knew. Ilkka returned to Oslo to do other things. When I was arrested for manslaughter, he would not have contact with me: He was afraid the police would ask questions and learn about the Jólasveinar sacrifices. Ilkka left the country, and when I was released I had no more reason to be there, so I came back to Niceland."

He went to the table where he'd set the Speed Graphic, picked it up, and turned it gently in his hands. I could see a fine line across the blue flashbulb that Ilkka had hoarded for so long, for nothing. After all that time and care, the fragile glass had finally been damaged.

"It was Ilkka's idea," Galdur said, and stared at the camera. "That we should resanctify the Jólasveinar. He had such great passion for many things. Every day for the last fifteen years, I have thought of him."

Pétur glanced at me, then at Galdur. "So you didn't kill him?"

"Why would I kill him?" Galdur retorted angrily. "How could I kill him? I have not left here in months. And Ilkka would not speak to me. I have not seen him in all this time!"

He stepped to the pile of rocks in the center of the room, bent, and placed Ilkka's camera directly behind the sunstone. I could see the reflector's eye staring back at me through the clouded crystal, its flawed iris a darker blue than it had been, almost violet. "'We know that love will be reborn,'" he recited softly, "'that death holds its own marvels, that both worlds hold joy.'"

For several minutes no one spoke. I touched my nose gingerly, drew away a finger flecked with blood. Then I picked up my leather jacket and withdrew the photo I'd hidden in the lining. I stared at it, then handed it to Galdur.

"Remember this guy?" He looked at the photo, his mouth grim. "Who was he?"

"This is the basement at Forsvar. I don't know his name. Someone who owed Anton money."

"That's Anton?" I pointed to the stocky man with thinning hair. Galdur nodded. "Who are the others?"

"Ilkka Kaltunnen. Brynja Ingvarsdottir. Myself. Quinn O'Boyle." His ran a finger across one of the shadowy forms. "Nils Pederson."

"What happened to him?"

"He hanged himself a few months later."

"Why was Quinn there?"

"He was there because Anton paid him." Galdur rested his hands upon his knees and bowed his head, as though praying. "Quinn disposed of things for him."

"Like this guy?"

"Among others."

"Is this when you made the tape?" He nodded. "Why? Why would you make a recording of something like that?"

"Ilkka thought we should. As a ritual, but also as a competitive thing, he thought, with some of the others in the scene. To prove we'd really done a blood sacrifice. I was the one who thought we should use it on the track. We only played it that once, in the studio, and then Ilkka destroyed the tape."

"He didn't destroy it. He kept it in his darkroom. I didn't know what it was; I took it and then I played it in Einar's car."

Pétur stood. "This is crazy. This conversation, both of you . . ." He shot me a desperate look. "*You* know these people too? Maybe you killed them all, right? Maybe that's why you're here now."

"He set you up," I said slowly, and looked at Galdur. "Your brother. That's why your passport disappeared. He needed money. Ilkka or Anton told him about the deal for the photos; he killed them and took the cash and the photos. Did he know about the Jólasveinar?"

Galdur's eyes widened. "Yes. I told him, once, a long time ago. A year or so after this all happened. Einar and I had been drinking. It was before I went to prison. He was the only one I ever told, because . . . he is my brother. I wanted someone to understand."

"Yeah, well, he understood, all right." I walked over to the skull lantern and stared into its guttering flame. "He had your passport and used it when he went to Oslo and Helsinki four days ago. Even if he didn't need it to travel, he could flash it around and someone would have a record that you'd been there. You look enough alike. I don't know what he did to Baldur; but the others, he set it up like one of your Yule guys. He broke Suri's neck in the door, and I guess he took her hand, because . . ."

I looked at Galdur questioningly.

"Because he's a fucking freak," said Pétur.

"He knew it would work." Galdur stared at the skull lantern and then at the stone altar. "The police would come here and see all these things and remember that I was in prison, also some other events."

"Were there tire tracks outside?" Pétur asked, and walked to the window and peered out. "Now it's snowing hard."

"I saw no tracks. But the wind would have covered them." said Galdur. "She left no tracks, either."

"'Winter swallows everything,'" I said. I got the bottle of Focalin from my bag and popped three of them dry. "That's what Ilkka told me."

"You spoke with him?"

"Yeah. That was the whole point of this enterprise—to look at his photos. Anton wanted my eye." I laughed. "He got the whole shooting match."

"What did you tell him? Not Anton—what did you tell *Ilkka*?"

I looked at Galdur, and for a second saw the same boy Ilkka must have known, long blond hair framing a face so beautiful and fraught with expectation that I had to turn away.

"I told him they were amazing," I said at last. "The most beautiful photos I've ever seen."

Galdur was silent. He took my chin in his hand, tilted my head, and gazed at me, his finger tracing the scar beside my eye and the open wound left by the raven. "You have his eyes," he said.

He let go of me and sank back onto the couch. "Einar has betrayed everyone he ever knew."

I sighed. "Well, he thinks on his feet, I'll tell you that. He dumped me out there, dumped my stuff in your Econoline, and hightailed it back to Reykjavík. Would he know Pétur was here with you?"

"Why should he? We don't talk. Pétur's car is parked in back; probably Einar didn't see it there. So . . ."

Galdur clapped his hands and stood. "I have an alibi. Lots of alibis," he added with a glance at me.

"You'll need them." Pétur turned from the window, his face grim. "Because someone is coming."

23

I ran to the window behind Galdur and peered through the filthy glass. Between grime and the snow swirling around outside, it was like staring into a cement mixer. I saw no one. Then with a screech of wind the door flew open. Something hit the floor—something big—then rolled over to stare at me with blood-swollen eyes.

It was Quinn. One side of his face was livid blue; a deep, up-curved gash sliced through the Inuit tattoo, as though someone had tried to carve a grotesque smile. I knelt beside him, frantically wiped snow and blood from his battered cheek as he whispered my name.

"Cassie. Don't—"

"*Villast!* Get lost, move—!"

A voice shouted as Pétur grabbed me and I stumbled to my feet. The shouting grew panicked; Pétur staggered back as someone lashed out at him.

"*What the hell is she doing here? Who are you?*"

"Einar." Galdur's deep rumble echoed beside me. "Einar, you must leave here now."

"Leave?" Einar kicked the door shut, then stepped over Quinn, clutching a gun with both hands. "No, Jonas—"

Galdur turned swiftly. "Pétur, go—"

"*Nei.*" Einar grabbed Pétur and pulled him to his side, jamming the gun against his temple. "Move, Jonas! I will kill him!"

I backed across the dim room until I bumped against the stone altar. Galdur stood his ground, Einar screaming at him in Icelandic until Pétur gasped, "For Christ's sake, Galdur!"

"What are you doing, Einar?" Galdur spoke quietly as he stepped toward the couch. "Why are you here? Do you need money? You know I have no money."

"Shut up!" Einar turned to me, his eyes huge. Blood seeped from his mouth; the hand grasping the gun trembled as though palsied. "How are you alive?" He sounded terrified.

"I will kill you," Galdur said calmly.

"No. No, no, Jonas, no you won't." Einar spoke as though comforting a child. He hugged Pétur to him and slid the gun's barrel into the boy's ear. "You'll have a lot of company."

I crouched beside the cairn and its bizarre offerings—Viking artifacts, antique camera, sunstone, cell phone. Reykjavík CSI would have fun with this one.

"What are you doing?" Einar edged toward me, dragging Pétur with him. I grabbed the cell phone and he laughed. "Yes, please, call 112! Or take a picture!"

I leaned away from the cairn and held the phone at arm's length. Across the room, I saw Quinn lying on the floor, head turned to stare at me. In the near-darkness he was the only thing I could see clearly, faint light pooling on that broken face with its corpselike grin, his bruised eyes inseparable from the shadows.

It is our gaze that keeps them alive.

I forced myself to look away. I opened the cell phone and pointed it at the violet iris in the center of the Speed Graphic's silver eye. I turned my head, squeezed my eyes shut, and pressed Call.

Within each of those old flashbulbs is an entire hidden universe. A wire filament coated with priming chemical, surrounded by shreds of magnesium or aluminum foil or wire, all poised within the pure oxygen that replaces air before the bulb is finally sealed. Current flows from the battery to the filament and ignites the foil, causing a miniature combustion, the magnesium or aluminum burning at the white-hot temperature that releases half a million lumens. Another heat source or spark can sometimes set it off, if you're not careful; even something as innocuous as a cell phone.

And that combustion is powerful enough for the bulb to explode. In an intact bulb, a protective lacquer coating keeps this from happening. Some bulbs were even manufactured so that they'd change color to indicate they'd been damaged and were therefore too dangerous to use.

Like this one.

I heard a click, a thump, Pétur's strangled cry. The room erupted into a blossoming, blinding radiance magnified by the sunstone. Splintered glass flew everywhere, as though a demonic hive had been disturbed. Shading my eyes, I dove across the cairn and crashed against Einar. He fell with a shout. There was an echoing retort, a second burst of light, as I was thrown aside. I clapped my hand to my neck, felt blood seeping through my fingers, and pried out a tiny shard of glass.

"Are you all right?" I nodded as Pétur helped me to my feet. He pointed at the swinging kerosene lantern behind us. "That was lucky; it didn't break."

I looked around for Quinn. He'd managed to pull himself up

and leaned against the door, staring, dazed, at the shadowy figure that towered above Einar's prostrate form.

"I swear, it was a mistake." Einar tried to stand, and Galdur kicked him. "Please, Jonas, you must listen—Jonas, I am begging you—"

Galdur's topaz eyes glittered as he stared at his brother, unblinking.

"Jonas is not here," he said. He turned, and I froze as he fixed that terrible gaze on me. "Strip him, then bind him," he commanded, indicating Einar, then raised his hand so that I could see he held the gun. "Now."

I scrabbled around the room, searching for a rope, until Galdur shouted angrily and tossed something at me—the jumper cables. He turned to yell at Pétur. "Help her!"

Pétur blanched. "What?"

"Do as I say."

I grabbed Pétur. "Better listen to him," I hissed. Einar fought us, screaming, and Galdur stooped to grab him by the hair.

"You are a craven animal," he said, and slammed his brother's head against the floor. "You have shamed your family and your country. You are a coward and a thief who has stolen so that your own people now go hungry."

"You're insane," Einar gasped. "You know I lost everything! I'm your fucking brother."

"I have no brother."

Galdur stepped back. After Pétur and I finally managed to tug off Einar's clothes, Galdur turned his brother's pockets inside out. He held up one set of car keys and then another and pocketed both, along with a thick leather wallet and a passport. Einar sprawled naked on the floor between us. His skin was white and slack, creased with red where he'd worn pants a size too small, his toes mashed-looking from the expensive leather shoes that had provided no protection from the snow and sleet.

I glanced at Pétur. He was pale, his expression a grim, younger reflection of Galdur's, cold and implacable as the stars. I fumbled with the jumper cables, and at last managed to tie a noose around Einar's hands. I tightened this and got unsteadily to my feet. Galdur picked up his brother's bespoke dress shirt, pulling the collar taut to read the label.

"How much did this cost?" Einar didn't respond. Galdur tore the shirt into strips and handed one to me. "This animal has lost the power of speech. Bind his mouth."

When I was finished, Galdur dragged Einar to his feet and pushed him past Quinn, toward the door. "Pétur. Bring the lantern. You, Cassandra—" He pointed at my camera. "And you, Varsler—"

He turned to Quinn. "I will need you again as well. All of you, come."

He strode outside, hauling Einar with him. I grabbed my coat, found a parka hanging on the wall and handed it to Quinn, then looked at Pétur. "Varsler—what does that mean?"

"Shrike." Pétur set down the lantern and pulled on his coat. He no longer looked dazed, more like someone who'd decided maybe the Kool-Aid didn't taste so bad after all. "The butcher bird, which impales other birds on thorn trees."

He zipped his parka, following Galdur into the snow. I glanced at Quinn beside me. "Are you okay? Can you do this?"

"Do I have a fucking choice?"

He walked haltingly, the two of us stepping into a trail of footprints that led away from the Quonset hut and into the darkness, toward the eerie columns of steam that rose above the horizon. I saw Quinn's Cherokee pulled behind the Econoline, its doors hanging open.

"What happened?" I asked in a low voice.

Quinn tugged at his parka's hood and grabbed my hand. When he spoke, flecks of frozen blood mingled with the snow around his face, silver and black. "I went to Kolaportið, but Baldur never showed up. He didn't answer his phone. No one there had seen him. I must've talked to a hundred people. No one had seen him all day. And you know, he's not a guy who's easy to miss.

"Then I got a call that they'd found him. He'd been murdered. Cops found some kind of old whale-oil lantern; whoever did it broke the chimney and just sawed away at his throat with a piece of glass."

His eyes filled. "No one would hurt Baldur. It makes no fucking sense. I drove to the shop, but you were gone, Brynja was gone. All I could think of was that text message we got from Anton, about Galdur; I thought Galdur must've totally gone off the deep end. So I started driving here; I was here once before, years ago. And of course I had no clue what happened to you; I thought you must be with Brynja and the cops. I followed Highway 35 and kept going, turned off onto the track in the highlands. After a couple hours I see headlights coming at me. I thought it was a snowmobile. Car passes me; I don't get a good look at it in the snow. Next thing I know the car does a one-eighty. I look in my rearview mirror and there's a fucking Range Rover wailing up behind me, and then it's ramming me. I'm trying to grab my gun out of the glove box. The Range Rover slams the Jeep and it skids into a ravine. Range Rover comes right after me, only it ends up on its roof. Then someone's dragging me through the snow, and it's fucking Einar Broddursson. He's screaming at me, 'What are you doing here?' Like I could ask you the same goddamn thing, asshole."

He spat, and a clot of blood bloomed on the snow at his feet. "Anton told him about you and those photos, Cassie. In Helsinki, before Einar killed him. I got the whole story. He was still in touch with Anton; they had various investments. Anton let something slip about the photos and some deal with Ilkka. And you. That's why Einar was dogging you: He saw you at Viva Las Vegas and then Kolaportið; he thought you were tailing him. Which would have been easy. He was so fucking sloppy. If I'd done that job for Anton, he would've fired me. Anyway, I'm a little shook up from the accident, so when Einar comes crawling out of his car like a spider, he takes me down in a heartbeat. Grabs my gun, pistol-whips me. Next thing I know, I'm here." He shook his head in disgust. "A fucking banker. Note that his Range Rover is still in that ravine."

"Why do they call you Varsler?"

"Because of the work I did for Anton." He looked away. "It was business, Cass. And it was a long time ago. Anton knew a lot of guys in Moscow. Same syndicate he fixed Einar up with, back when his bank started looking for new investment opportunities. Trust me, none of these were people you'd invite for dinner."

"Were they the same people Ilkka photographed?"

"No. That was Galdur's thing, and Ilkka's. Another one of their private rituals. I know nothing about any of that shit."

He fell silent. A golden blister bulged above the serrated ridge of mountains to the east, moonrise above the waste of ice and charred stone. Vortices of snow leapt from the frozen ground to accompany us, uncanny escorts that would suddenly collapse into glittering clouds blown away by the wind. In the near distance, two black figures materialized from the smoke, a third shadow suspended between them.

"Why would Einar kill Baldur?"

"I have no fucking idea. Maybe he wanted to frame me."

"'Help Galdur,'" I said. "It meant we should help him. It wasn't a warning."

"No." Quinn stared at the three forms silhouetted in the moonlight, his expression bleak. "But I gotta tell you, right now I don't think Galdur needs a lot of help."

A ledge of cloud obscured the moon, save for a shining rift that ran parallel with the horizon and glowed astral white. Below this, columns of steam jetted into the air. We were now close enough that I could see a variegated network of pools within rocky clefts, some big enough to swallow a house, others so small I could have jumped across them.

Not that I'd want to try. Huge bubbles and glistening froth broke the surface, which simmered as though something vast and angry breathed beneath. The falling snow evaporated into wisps of steam sucked into the boiling columns that erupted from the largest pools. It all had a rich mineral smell that, weirdly, made my mouth water—not just sulfur but charcoal, copper, salt, the hot reek of the Earth's own blood spurting up everywhere around us.

I stopped to crouch beside a trickle of water that emerged from a thumb-size cleft in the rock. Iridescent mud surrounded it, slicks of acid green and cobalt and cadmium yellow, colors I'd never seen before in the natural world. But of course this is where pigments come from, disgorged from the center of the planet to cool into vermilion and lapis lazuli. I held my hand above the fuming vent, gingerly dipped my finger into the water, and snatched it back.

"Shit." I straightened, sucking on my fingertip, and held it out to Quinn. It had already blistered.

"You never learn," he said.

He looked to where the others had stopped at the edge of a pool, its far shore lost in the biochemical haze. Einar was on his knees, head weaving blindly back and forth as Galdur stared into the mist. Pétur glanced at us furtively. I suspected that, in the future, Reykjavík's nightlife was going to seem very dull to him.

"Quinn." Galdur's voice echoed above the susurrus of boiling springs. "Come here. And you, Cassandra."

Beneath my boots the soft ground gave off heat: It was like walking across a giant body. Galdur was speaking to Pétur in a low voice. As we drew alongside them he glanced at us and nodded, then reached down to grasp Einar by the arm.

"Stand up," he commanded. He looked at Pétur. "Remember, unlike this one, you are a man," he said, and turned to me. "I am not certain what you are. But—" He pointed at my eyes, then at the Konica slung around my neck. "Use them."

I nodded, grabbed my flash from my pocket, and screwed it on; I took a step back, praying the steam wouldn't cloud my lens, and popped the lens cap. Pétur stepped beside Einar and grabbed one end of the jumper cable, pulling it until Einar stood upright. Galdur reached into his pocket and withdrew a bright coil—the broken guitar string. He unwound it, several feet of 11-gauge stainless steel.

You need big hands to control a string that size. Galdur had them. So did Quinn. Galdur bowed his head slightly at Quinn, his long hair falling forward to expose a tattoo on the back of his neck: three skeletal hands, a Möbius loop where past, present, future clutched one another in a death grip. He handed the guitar string to Quinn.

"When I tell you," said Galdur.

He removed his anorak and flannel shirt, tossed them a safe distance from the boiling pool. He let his head fall back and gazed up into the sky, an opening in the roil of steam and cloud where a swath of stars appeared, at their center the brilliant triad of Orion's belt.

"Baldur Enriksson. Anton Bredahl. Suri Kulmala..." Galdur turned, his tear-streaked face still lifted to the sky, and shouted a final name. "Ilkka Kaltunnen."

He raised his clenched fist and grasped it with his right hand and began to sing, the words unrecognizable but their meaning clear: a litany of grief and rage and longing, his deep voice rising to a wail of despair and fading to a hoarse rattle, before it swelled once more to join the echoes that rang from the mountain peaks, an unseen host of voices mourning, then shouting in triumph as Galdur drew his hands apart and raised them to the sky.

" 'Brothers shall slay each other; our land weeps with suffering.' " Behind me I heard Quinn half chanting under his breath. " 'The whore's sons bleed the earth, wolf-time, wolf-years. The wolf runs free until Viðar fetters its jaws. Then Baldur returns, and the sun like gold.' "

Galdur turned to Quinn. "*Nú*," he said.

Quinn stepped directly behind Einar, as though to embrace him. He lifted his hands and tightened the glimmering strand between them. A faint note sounded, then faded into a sharp intake of breath as Quinn stepped back and drew the cord across Einar's throat, his hands moving so quickly I saw only a scythe of light and then a black tongue of blood lapping at Einar's chest. I jammed my camera's viewfinder against my face and started shooting.

Einar's head lolled forward, knees buckling as the body folded in upon itself then fell to the ground. I cursed as the roll of film ran out, straightened, and wiped my eyes. Quinn knelt beside the body, quickly undid the jumper cable, then tugged the steel wire from where it had lodged in Einar's windpipe. Galdur came up beside him, grabbed Quinn's shoulder, roughly yanked him to his feet, then pushed him toward me.

"Don't look," Quinn said, pulling me with him.

I shook him off. I watched as Galdur grasped Einar's lower jaw in one huge hand, jammed his fingers behind the upper jaw, then wrenched them apart.

"Fucking hell." I gasped as Quinn hugged me close. "Who the hell does that?"

"Viðar," said Pétur in an unsteady voice. "That is how he kills the Fenrir Wolf at Ragnarök."

"Remind me to be out of town that weekend." My hands shook as I replaced the lens cap and stuffed the flash into my jacket. I looked at Quinn. "Jesus Christ, Quinn."

"What'd I say, Cassie? You and those big gray eyes." He stepped to the edge of the hot spring and dropped one end of the guitar string into it. He dragged it through the simmering water as though it were a fishing line, pulled it out, and began coiling it. "The world will end and you won't blink."

I turned to see Galdur standing beside Pétur. He lowered his head, speaking softly. After a moment Pétur nodded, eyes squeezed shut as Galdur pressed his thumb against his forehead, leaving a bloody mark. Galdur turned, stepped over to Quinn, and did the same to each of us.

"Because you are part of this now, too," he said.

He returned to Einar's corpse, stooped and picked it up, slinging it over his shoulder as though it were a sack, and walked to the edge of the hot spring. Several large rocks protruded from the simmering water; Galdur stepped carefully from one to the next, his form swathed in steam. Near the center of the pool he halted, leaned forward, and let the body slide into the murk. There was no sound, only an upward surge of boiling water as Galdur quickly retraced his steps. As he walked toward us, he picked up his flannel shirt, paused to dip it into the boiling water, then sluiced it across his chest. He wrung out the shirt and tossed it to Quinn, who went to the water's edge and used it to clean his hands and face before passing it to Pétur, who did the same.

"I think I'm good," I said when Pétur turned to me. I wiped the smear of blood from my forehead and followed the others to the Quonset hut. When I glanced back, I saw a small black shape circling lazily above the steaming pool before it settled several yards from the edge and folded its wings to wait.

24

No one spoke when we got back inside. Pétur went into the bedroom and shut the door. Galdur opened a bottle of wine and tipped it to his mouth, swallowing more than half the bottle before he handed what remained to Quinn.

"It is a long history that is over now, I think," he said in his bass rumble. He looked exhausted, about twenty years older than he had a few hours ago. "From that time, not many of us are left."

Quinn took a pull from the wine and passed it to me. "Are you sorry?"

"That Einar is dead?" Galdur shook his head. "No. And that time is gone. But I am sorry for the friends I lost."

He stared at the ceiling, then stood and gently pulled down the photograph of himself and Ilkka. "That was at Vitenskapsmuseet, the archaeological museum in Trondheim. Ilkka knew someone there, a curator. She took this picture. It was a few weeks after he and I first met at Helvete."

He gazed at the photo, his topaz eyes damp, and set it aside. He glanced at the closed bedroom door. "I need to talk to Pétur. I will say farewell to you now."

He stood. I glanced at Quinn and took a step after Galdur.

"Anton owed me money. From when I went to meet with Ilkka. He paid me half up front, and he was going to send the rest to New York. Do you know what happened to it?"

Galdur reached into his back pocket and withdrew Einar's wallet, opened it to display a wad of five-hundred-euro notes. "How much money?"

"Ten thousand euros. But that can't be all of it." I pointed at the wallet. "He—"

Galdur peeled off some bills and handed them to me, counted out more and put them into his pocket. "I will give you five. This I will keep. I know a man who needs to buy a new whaling boat for himself and his son." He stared at me. "It is time now for you to leave. First, please give me that film."

"The film?"

He pointed at my camera. "The photos you took out there. I want them."

"But—you asked me to take those!"

"Yes. And now they are mine."

He extended his hand. I looked at Quinn, who only raised his eyebrows and nodded slightly. Swearing under my breath, I retreated to a dark corner, removed the roll from the camera, and handed it to Galdur.

"*Takk.*" He gathered Einar's clothes from the floor, picked up Ilkka's six prints, and headed for the door. "Come. I'll get you some petrol."

Quinn and I followed him outside. It had stopped snowing. Above us the sky stretched black and scoured of stars. We waited as Galdur walked to the Econoline and returned with a plastic gasoline container. He tossed the clothes onto the snow-covered ground, poured gas on them, then set the pile alight with a match. As the flames rose from the little pyre, he tossed the roll of film onto it, then one by one, Ilkka's photos. I barely resisted the urge to snatch them from the blaze and watched, my gut tightening, as the sparks whirled upward, a thousand tiny constellations that flared then died along with Ilkka's legacy. And mine.

When the embers cooled, Galdur kicked snow across an oily black smear, all that remained of the Jólasveinar sequence. He handed the gas can to Quinn, who headed to the Cherokee to fill the tank.

"Here." Galdur turned to me. He took my hand, opened it, and pressed something into my palm, then closed my fingers around it. "This is the one that Ilkka used when he took those photos: He set his flash so it would bounce off the crystal. He would have wanted you to have it, I think."

I opened my hand to see a polished lump of dark blue crystal, winking in the starlight. "It is his *solstenen*, his 'sunstone,'" Galdur went on. "I think perhaps you might need it sometimes, Valkyrie, to see your way in the dark."

"*Takk*," I said, and held it tight inside my fist.

"We're set." Quinn stopped beside me and handed the empty can back to Galdur. "Thanks."

Galdur set the can down. He clasped his wrist and raised it in a salute. Quinn returned it, and the two men embraced.

"I need to be with Pétur," said Galdur as he turned to go. "I have my passport back now, and some money. . . . Perhaps we will visit Rome."

We watched him go inside, then headed for the Cherokee. Quinn slung his arm around my shoulder. "Tough luck about your photos, Cassie."

"Yeah." I thought of the clandestine pictures I'd shot of Quinn while he was sleeping and rubbed my eyes. "Some bad fucking shit there. But I wasn't going to arm-wrestle him over it."

"Good idea."

I gave him some Focalin, and we drove the five hours back to Quinn's place, where we took turns showering, fell into bed for a few hours, then slept. When I woke, Quinn sat beside me, stroking my hair.

"I made you a reservation on the night flight to London." I began to protest, and he pressed his hand against my mouth, then held up a red passport. "I'm giving you this. It's Dagny's. I figure if Einar can pass himself off as Galdur, you can pass for her."

"I'm not Swedish!"

"I know. But listen to me. You can't stay here, and you say you're fucked if you go back to New York. And maybe you get stopped at Keflavik, but probably they're just gonna glance at this and let you through. At Heathrow they're all gonna speak English, so just try to fake an accent. Find a cheap hotel and e-mail me. I'll find you in a couple of days, a week tops. There's a bar in Brixton run by someone I know; I'll give you his number. I'll meet you there. What do you say?"

"Shit." I rubbed my head, finally nodded. "Yeah, I guess. You'll meet me there? Really?"

He leaned toward me till our foreheads touched. "Really. I didn't go through all that shit just to kiss you on the runway and wave good-bye."

"What happens when we get to London?"

"We'll burn that bridge when we get to it. C'mon, get your stuff."

It'd been a long time since I cried, but I came close when we got to Keflavik. Quinn went with me into the airport, walked me to security, then gathered me in his arms.

"We'll always have Reykjavík," he whispered.

"Fucking A." I punched him gently, then pulled away. "I'll see you in London."

I watched him as I went up the escalator, the gray overhead light shadowing the grim lines on his face and that grotesque, scarred half smile. He raised his hand, clasped his wrist in farewell, and was gone.

The flight was nearly empty. I got a window seat, popped a Percocet, and chased it with the Jack Daniel's minis I'd bought at duty free. I was just starting to drift off when I heard excited voices. I looked up to see the flight attendants clustered around a bulkhead window, staring out and pointing. I pressed my face against my own window, looked down, and saw the vast white expanse that was Iceland, with its ragged black hem of ocean. A red eye boiled within the snowy wilderness, its flaming iris surrounded by a plume of gray and black.

"A volcano!" One of the flight attendants peered over my shoulder. "It's just erupted, see? A thousand years ago, the first monks saw that and thought it was the gates of Hell opening for them."

"I can relate," I said, and reached for another whiskey.

About the author

Elizabeth Hand is the bestselling author of fourteen genre-spanning novels and five collections of short fiction and essays. Her work has received multiple Shirley Jackson, World Fantasy and Nebula Awards, among other honors, and several of her books have been *New York Times* and *Washington Post* Notable Books.

Acknowledgments

As ever, eternal gratitude to my agent, Martha Millard, for her support and encouragement over the years.

To Marcia Markland and Kat Brzozowski of Thomas Dunne Books, for all their help in bringing this book to light.

To Bob Morales, who came up with the title.

To my friends in Finland, Kati Makki-Clements and Tino Warinowski, for assistance with all things Suomi.

To Professor K. A. Laity, for her invaluable advice regarding all things Icelandic and *Kalevala*.

To Jonathan Clements, very special thanks for advising me on the finer linguistic points of Finnish, Icelandic, and Old Norse, as well as for his insights into shamanism and ancient Nordic ritual.

To David Shaw, Eric Van, and Robert Wexler, for sharing their knowledge of Nordic music, as well as to everyone who posted helpful info on *The Inferior 4 + 1* blog.

To Jonathan Clements, Ellen Datlow, Kate Laity, Bob Morales, and Bill Sheehan, who read this book in manuscript.

To John Clute, who traveled to Iceland with me in 2009, with all my love.

Finally, in memory of my lifelong friend, Russell Dunn, whose longtime dream was to visit Iceland, and who was my comrade-in-arms during my first trip to that country in 2007. "We know that love will be reborn, that death holds its own marvels, that both worlds hold joy." Farewell, old friend.

"A literary page-turner.deeply pleasurable. Hand's lushly worded tale is consistently gripping. . . . A delightful waking dream."
— *People*

"A wonderfully Gothic atmosphere, with lush visual imagery and rich poetic language." — *Library Journal*

"Mortal Love is bewitching, sexy, creepy and, under all, dazzlingly romantic." — *Detroit Free Press*

ebook · 9781618730831

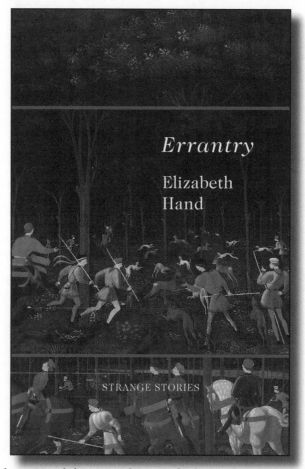

Errantry

Elizabeth Hand

STRANGE STORIES

"At her best, Hand does just this: We find ourselves wrapped in an evocation without knowing fully how she got us there, shivering with fear at an image of lights or blinking with awe at the modest beauty of a small, rare creature living its life, seen from a distance."
—Aimee Bender, *Washington Post*

"No writer has cornered the market on darkly beautiful, unsettling stories. But it's a niche that Elizabeth Hand inhabits with uncanny ease." —*Maine Sunday Telegram*

Shirley Jackson Award finalist

paper · $16 · 9781618730305 | ebook · 9781618730312

"A startling and addictive novel that introduced a protagonist fueled by drugs and post-punk irreverence."
— Danielle Trussoni, *New York Times Book Review*

"Hand's terse but transporting prose keeps the reader turning pages until Neary's gritty charm does, finally, shine through."
— *Entertainment Weekly*

Shirley Jackson Award winner

paper · $17 · 9781618731746 | ebook · 9781618730107

"This smart, dark, literary thriller will keep you up at night." — Megan Sullivan, *Boston Globe*

HARD LIGHT

ELIZABETH HAND

"This third novel in the Cass Neary series fades away as stubbornly as a bloodstain." — Maureen Corrigan, *The Washington Post*

"Nerve-jangling and addictive, Elizabeth Hand's *Hard Light* offers up a signature Cass Neary tale of moral ambivalence, keen betrayal and a dark lushness that leaps off the page. And with Cass—relentless in her dangerous curiosity, her ruthless art of survival—Hand has created an anti-hero for the ages. We'd follow her anywhere, into any glittery abyss, and do."
—Megan Abbott

"Elizabeth Hand's Cass Neary novels, rightly praised for their icy tension and remarkable darkness, are threaded, like the best of punk in any medium, on a bloodied yet admirably stubborn humanism." —William Gibson "

paper · $17 · 9781618731920 | ebook · 9781618731937